Julien Parme

Julien Parme

FLORIAN ZELLER

translated by
William Rodarmor

OTHER PRESS • NEW YORK

Ouvrage publié avec le concours du Ministère français chargé de la culture–Centre national du Livre.

We wish to express our appreciation to the French Ministry of Culture–CNL for its assistance in the preparation of the translation.

Originally published as *Julien Parme* by Florian Zeller.

Production Editor: Robert D. Hack

Text design: Natalya Balnova
This book was set in 11.8pt Bembo by Alpha Graphics of Pittsfield, NH.

10 9 8 7 6 5 4 3 2 1

Library of Congress Cataloging-in-Publication Data

Zeller, Florian.
 Julien Parme / by Florian Zeller ; translated by William Rodarmor.
  p. cm.
 ISBN-13: 978-1-59051-280-7
 ISBN-10: 1-59051-280-4
 I. Rodarmor, William. II. Title.
 PQ2686.E469J813 2006
 843'.92–dc22

                                            2007031089

To Gabriel

It seemed reasonable and necessary to him, both for the sake of his honor and as a service to the nation, to become a knight errant and travel the world with his armor and his horse to seek adventures and engage in everything he had read that knights errant engaged in, righting all manner of wrongs and, by seizing the opportunity and placing himself in danger and ending those wrongs, winning eternal renown and everlasting fame.

—Miguel Cervantes, *Don Quixote de la Mancha*,
tr. Edith Grossman

Part 1

Preparations

Chapter 1

Even if it blows your mind, I want to tell you about this unbelievable thing that happened to me last year. I'm not bragging, but things as unbelievable as the one I'm going to tell you about don't happen every day, I swear. In fact, they never happen. That's why I'm talking about it. Because I'm not the kind of person who bullshits other people about my own life. It's a question of style. It's like this guy who was in my class then, his name was Antoine Cheval. A hell of a name, when you think of it. Well, you'd ask him a question about something—just to be polite, to acknowledge his existence and all—and that would be it, he'd chew your ear off for hours about his personal life. That kind of person has always made me sick. So when someone says he's got an unbelievable thing to tell you, I watch out. You can't ever let a guy who tells you that get started. Otherwise you're a goner: you'll have to listen to him right to the end.

But in my particular case, it's not the same thing since I'm the one telling it. Also, I'm not Antoine Cheval. With him, I

got taken in at first. I asked stuff like, "Where are you from?"
and, "What do you think about this?" to be nice, but basically
I didn't care. It was just that we sat next to each other in class.
I was new, since I had just gotten there from Paris. I mean, right
in the middle of the year. I had screwed up a little back home,
and they shipped me off to this shitty town in the East. Like a
kind of punishment. Didn't I tell you my mother was slightly
hysterical? I should have started with that. Because she was
really hysterical. Like all mothers, you might say. Except that
she was even more hysterical than a normally hysterical mother.
Super strict, no sense of humor or anything. There was no way
to have any fun with her. So of course I got chewed out all the
time. Honestly, it was no joke. Though now that I think of it,
I realize it was actually more the opposite: my mother wasn't
hysterical; she'd flickered out. Like a candle in a draft.

I was living in Paris with her and François, a jerk in a goatee
and corduroy pants. My father died of cancer when I was about
nine. She went out with a couple of guys afterward, and François
was the last one in a parade of losers. Anyway, after my screw-
ups, they wanted to send me to Nice, to my uncle's. That's
normal, you might say, that's what parents are for: all I had to
do was not screw up. But if you want to know the whole story,
I think my screw-ups were an excuse. Actually, they were glad
to get rid of me. I'd be one less thing to worry about. Things
would settle down, and they'd be living the good life. In a way,
they must've been really happy to have to punish me. They

claimed I hung out with a bad crowd in Paris, and besides, I was impressionable. Whatever. And it wasn't open for discussion. When my mother makes her mind up about something, best not to cross her.

Only, my uncle said no. That was too bad in a way, because he lives in a house by the sea. As a punishment, things could have been worse. All the rooms have balconies. You can see Italy in the distance. Italy is classy. Even from far away. But he said no. I didn't quite understand why. Supposedly he had to travel a lot that year, or something. So my mother didn't know how to get rid of me. That's when she decided to send me to a family friend who lives in the Vosges. I kid you not. The Vosges. Where it pours rain in the summer, and in winter it's worse than an icicle down your neck. I didn't even know that the Vosges still existed. That's saying something. But you're probably wondering, why not Siberia? while she was at it. The answer is simple: because my mother didn't know anybody there. As you can imagine, I tried everything to avoid it, but no dice. She and François stuck me on a train with a suitcase and it was off to Saint-Dié. That's how it all began. Or rather that's how it all ended.

Why am I telling you all this? Oh yeah, because of Antoine Cheval. When I got to Saint-Dié, he didn't have a study partner. He was the only one who didn't have a study partner. Kinda made you think nobody wanted to sit next to a guy like him. In any case, no one feels like making friends with someone like

Antoine Cheval. That's why I wound up talking with him. Because I landed there in the middle of the year and there was only one free seat left in the damned classroom. Dumb Cheval wouldn't quit telling me about his life. I couldn't stand it. Especially because he always focused on boring details like birth dates and so on. He must have thought I came to the Vosges just to write his biography, like in ten volumes. What he said was such a drag, it almost made me want to listen to the teacher. That's telling you something. That's the way Cheval was; he'd get carried away about nothing. "You know what I saw on TV yesterday?" he'd ask. And he's off to the races. Seriously. A total idiot.

He reminded me of François. That one was a case, too. I wonder where my mother found him. In an antique store, I bet. The only thing I knew about him was that he was from a noble family, with a "de" in his name, a *particule*. De Courtois. That seemed really important to him, being François *de* Courtois. I thought it was pretty dumb, myself. Maybe if it came with a castle or something. But a "de" isn't anything to get all fired up about. But he was exactly the kind of person to get fired up over crap like that. He probably looked in the mirror every morning and said, "I have a *particule!*" The guy talked about himself nonstop. He always did it in front of guests, for example. They'd barely be seated on the living-room sofa when François would start talking about himself, about his particule, telling his family stories. It was his favorite subject. Like the fact that he was related to some guy who wound up having his head cut off. That was no reason to bore the rest of us out of our skulls.

I don't get guys like that. It kills me. No kidding, I can't stand it. I won't play along. Because the guests usually sort of had to play along. Since they were guests. They'd listen, nod, shift in their seats, discreetly look at their watches, or say, "Uh-huh . . . Uh-huh . . . I understand, that's amazing . . ." So they would play the game. But me, I'd never play along. Sometimes I'd completely cover my ears. Or else I'd go to another room to make it clear that I couldn't care less about his family stories. That's what I mean when I say I want to tell you something unbelievable: I'm not the kind of person to get fired up about bullshit.

In fact, the so-called family friend, the woman in the Vosges who was supposed to take me in, was actually from François's family. I really couldn't see what the hell I was doing in Saint-Dié. In the beginning, it was mainly the name I thought was weird. Saint-Dié. As a first name, Dié is really pathetic. "Hello, I'd like you to meet Dié!" It's crazy to think that a mother could be so clueless as to call her son Dié. Didier is bad enough, but Dié . . . Mothers just don't get it. They always do just anything at all, and sometimes even on purpose. Anyway. But I don't want to come across as a guy who's always complaining, especially about this. I mean when it comes to a first name, I have to admit I'm lucky. My name is Hughes. No, I'm kidding, my name is Julien. With my last name, it makes Julien Parme. That's style. Haven't you ever heard of Julien Parme? The great writer? No?

Really? Because I forgot to tell you that I want to be a great writer. Okay. If my name were Dié, for example, I think I'd have to change it. For my books. I'd choose Julien instead, so it would make "Julien Parme." So it all works out okay, since that's already my name.

Actually where it all began was the day where they stuck me on the train. The whole business sucked. What especially killed me was the feeling that they wanted to get rid of me. First my mother, then my uncle. In short, nobody wanted to have me around. They thought I was hopeless. And especially on the train platform, I could feel that my mother was telling herself: "All right, just hang in there a little longer, and the nightmare will be over." What made me crazy was that she didn't even look sad. In her defense it should be said that my mother didn't have an easy life. Protestant upbringing and all. I won't tell you all the details of her life. Let's just say she had a bunch of tough times. Lousy stuff. My father's illness, for example. Which is why she was pretty burned out. And she didn't know how to smile anymore.

In any case I was having trouble smiling too, that day, the day of the train. I was majorly depressed. And to make sure they realized I was depressed, I didn't answer the questions they were asking me. I was stone faced—heroic, nothing can touch me. But deep down I almost felt like bawling. Notice I didn't say I felt like bawling. No; I'm only saying I *almost* felt like it. That's not the same thing. After all, I wasn't a kid anymore. I'd be fifteen soon. In a year.

In any case when it comes to atmosphere, train stations have never been my thing. All those people saying good-bye and crying about it, that always brings me down. Especially on a really cold day like that one, with the rain coming down outside. A Sunday, too. I'd be starting classes the next day, in the only boarding school that was willing to take me in the middle of the year. No, honestly, it was enough to make you go hang yourself in your underwear. Still, my mother had bought me a new suitcase. It was huge, with wheels and all. To store all my things. In fact, I had taken almost everything I had. I'd applied the scorched-earth technique to my bedroom in Paris, and it looked like a cemetery. Because in my mind my parents would never see me again, I packed as much stuff as I could in my bag. They didn't want me around anymore? Fine. I wouldn't bother them much longer. Not that I planned to live out my life in Saint-Dié. No thanks. I'm not crazy. I know the provinces: I've been there, and they're not my thing. But when I got back to Paris there'd be no question of knocking on their door. I'd manage. I'd make my life without them. No kidding. I wouldn't be the first person to do it.

That day, the day of the train, I kept telling myself that this was the last time I would see my mother. I repeated it to myself so it really sank in, and filled me with the idea that it was the end of something. The first part of my life. When life was just a bowl of cherries. Anyway, it hit me at the time. Like the day of a funeral, if you want a comparison. I already knew I would turn it into a chapter in one of my future novels. A very cruel chapter that would make people cry and all. I would call it "The Farewell." It would be the story of the hero who decides never to go home again, as revenge for his mother's cruelty. Something that would move people to tears. One day, a woman journalist would see it as the key to my entire oeuvre. She would come to interview me. I'd be smoking my cigar, and she'd be a little intimidated, of course. "Tell me, Monsieur Parme, do you agree that your entire masterful oeuvre is foreshadowed in this separation, which is described in a wrenching chapter that you subtly and pertinently call 'The Farewell'?" And I would answer something super intelligent that would just kill her. I don't know what yet, but something super intelligent. Bam! One more. She would look a little like Madame Thomas, my French teacher. After the interview we would go out to dinner, and as usual, we'd wind up in bed.

Madame Thomas was probably the only teacher I felt lousy about leaving. At least she knew how to make her classes interesting. She often wore sheer blouses. I used to wonder if it wasn't just to make us fantasize. When you wear sheer blouses, even if they're just a little transparent, you're aware of it, aren't you? In any case she was really beautiful. For a teacher, I mean. Young and all. She replaced the guy who was supposed to teach us, Monsieur Vigouse, who got very sick two weeks after school started. A total loser who tried to look cool by wearing cowboy boots. The guy was like two centuries behind the times. That's especially what made me feel sad about leaving my high school. Never seeing her again. Someday she'd be reading the newspaper and come across my picture in it with this written underneath: "Julien Parme wins Nobel Prize at 20." She would remember me. She'd feel moved, and really proud, of course. She'd go buy my book in a real bookstore right away and she'd read it that night to see if I mentioned her. And that's how she'd find out that I'd been in love with her.

In my novel there would also be a fairly harsh description of François. How that loser with the *particule* tried to help me lift my suitcase onto the train, for example. I told him flat out it was too heavy for him. François was the kind of guy who hadn't done any sports for at least fifty years. Maybe sixty. His body was all flabby from not doing anything all day long. Honestly, I wonder what my mother saw in him. Anyway, I handled my suitcase all by myself. I stowed it up high, above my seat, and checked to see that it was wedged in. For safety. Because if a suitcase like that fell on you it could kill you. Can't fool around with that. My mother and François were still on the platform. They were waiting for me to come say good-bye. For a moment I thought of taking my seat, just like that, without a word. It would have killed them. Them on the platform waiting for me and me in my seat. But I decided to come down from the train. My mother said she would give me a little money. I'd probably need it. Anyway, you just don't do that, not kiss your mother good-bye when you know it's the last time you're ever going to see her. So I went back. Suddenly I had a vision: there they were, the two of them, shivering on the platform, waiting for something. I suddenly had the impression that they were very old, really very old, with that lost look that really old people have, the ones in wheelchairs and all. I also had the feeling they were going to die soon. And I told myself that would be just as well. It gave me a chill down my spine.

My mother kissed me and said she hoped that this would give me something to think about. Fat chance. François gave me a little envelope. I knew what was in it, but I opened it anyway, to check. There were a few bills. Hardly anything. And a letter. Goddamn. I could already imagine what they had written me. More preaching. I stuffed it in my jacket pocket. It made me feel strange to be taking this money in front of them, just like that. After all the cash I'd swiped from them . . . Then I got back aboard the train. I was tempted to say something stupid like, "Saint-Dié's like the toilet: when you gotta go, you gotta go!" But I held back. I preferred to stay silent. So they could feel right up to the last minute that it was really crappy to be sending me away—cutting me off from my friends, from my life, and from Mathilde.

Then a sharp whistle rang out. It still echoes in my mind. And the train door closed automatically.

Chapter 2

I realize I forgot to tell you why they were sending me away. That's me all over, forgetting to say the important things. I have to tell you the whole story so you'll understand; otherwise you won't understand anything. You've probably already guessed that all this was mainly because of Mark Russo. Marco to his pals. He lived in a maid's room, top floor. A really nice setup with a view over the rooftops and all. His parents rented it for him because they weren't living in Paris then. It was sort of my dream. The idea of living alone, without parents on my back or anything. But I knew I had to put in three more years at least before I'd be at that point. All of high school, in other words. Provided I wasn't held back, which could happen, since I tended not to kill myself when it came to schoolwork. What was cool about Marco is that we could talk about anything. He knew a lot about girls, for example. He'd already slept with a few. So had I, of course, but that's another story.

Anyway, since the start of classes we'd been spending more and more time together. He was two years older than me, but was always being held back. That must have evened things out, but I don't know for sure.

Up to then I'd always been the worst fuck-up in all the schools I'd gone to. I didn't do a damn thing in class. If I wanted to, I could've gotten good grades, but I didn't want to. First because I'm stubborn, and once I decide something I rarely change my mind. And also because I couldn't see the point of it. At one time I was getting super-good grades. Easily, and no sweat. I was even near the top of my class. And then I suddenly decided to stop. It wasn't just to annoy my mother. It was also because I thought good grades were pointless. That's what I told myself each time I tried to hit the books. Take math, for example. Aside from the class grinds, who would soon be cubicled away in some office, what was math good for? Nothing. Take someone who wants to be a writer: What the hell does he care about getting a zero in math, since he knows he's going to write terrific books and that someday even his math teacher, that douchebag Monsieur Ladibe, will be impressed when he sees him in the street?

The problem was, my not studying really pissed my mother off. If you could have seen her, you would have been scared for me. Like I told you: Protestant upbringing and all. It was no joke. She said she didn't know what to do with me, and so forth. That's why she'd enrolled me in a private school. To make the story clearer, I should have started with that, the time when she enrolled me at the Institut. A place where they force-fed you work until the day of the baccalaureat exam. That's where I met Marco.

I didn't really like the school much. In fact I hated it. It felt like being in the Army. Actually, I'm almost sure they recruited some of our teachers in the barracks. They all looked like they were ready to start World War III. No kidding. And it was super strict, no fooling around or anything. That's what they tried for, anyway. Because actually we fooled around just as much there as anywhere else. But we heard about the rules from morning till night. If you didn't follow the rules to the letter you supposedly got unbelievable punishments. You had to watch your step. The one exception was Madame Thomas. She was really sweet. That's why I started to love French as a subject. In the beginning I had a really lousy vocabulary. I ended each sentence with "like." And my sentences were three words long, max, four with "like." Whereas at the end I wanted to be a writer, with cigars and interviews, and I was writing killer essays that blew everyone away.

But except for French, you could die standing up of an overdose of boredom. I felt I'd been thrown in jail. That's what I sometimes used to tell myself. For fun. I would hatch escape plans, since I was innocent. It was clear that the moment would come pretty soon when I'd vanish into thin air. I just had to be patient.

I still remember the day when everything fell apart. I was in Marco's room, where we often went after class. But this time, I was slumped in his armchair watching him get dressed up. I was hurting. Because I was really depressed that day. The reason was that, contrary to what had been planned, I wasn't going to be able to go out that evening. Even though we'd been talking about this party for ages. It would be the party of the year, according to Marco. Goddamn it. Actually it was the birthday of Emilie Fermat, a senior. She was a major hottie, if you must know. And everybody was fantasizing about her, because she'd appeared in a movie. An actress, in other words. I forget the name of the movie but people at the Institut talked about it every day since it came out. It wound up getting on your nerves. That's why I didn't want to go see it. So as not to be like other people. Afterward I changed my mind, when I found out that she showed her boobs in the movie. By then it wasn't playing anymore. Anyway, everybody had tried to get invited to this birthday party.

If you were a sophomore, like me, forget it. That's not surprising, in a way. But Marco had scored. Seriously. The explanation was that he'd already been held back 212 times and was almost the same age as Emilie Fermat. As proof, he would kiss her good-bye when our classes let out. That was the sort of thing that impressed most people. But it left me cold. Because I didn't give a damn about Emilie Fermat. The person who interested me more was her little sister Mathilde, who was also a sophomore but who I didn't dare speak to. When Mathilde Fermat looked you in the eyes, it gave you the shivers.

Marco had asked if I could come with him to the party, and Emilie had agreed. "I managed to squeeze you in," he told me, with the weary look of a guy who's just given you a free blood donation. He thought I'd be really happy to go to this girl's birthday, just because she was an actress and all, whereas in fact if I was happy, it was mainly about seeing Mathilde. Because I told myself she'd probably be there, too. It would be a chance to talk, to hang out a little. Their address was near the Champs-Élysées, and according to what Marco told me there'd be lots of actresses and all. "Like heaven on earth."

I was sick at not being able to go after all.

As a general rule, my mother would rather see me dead than let me go out on a weeknight. No kidding. Even on the weekend it was always like pulling teeth. I had to bullshit her. But I couldn't just tell her that I absolutely had to go to this party because it was Emilie Fermat's birthday, the actress who showed her boobs, and that there would be plenty of other actresses, and super gorgeous ones I bet, who also showed their boobs, since everyone knows all actresses wind up showing their boobs sooner or later.

As a general rule, asking my mother for something like that was a little like going bungee jumping without the bungee cord. Suicide, pure and simple. But I'd worked something out by telling her an impossible story. First I tried to present the thing to her in a really good light, like it was an evening organized to fight world hunger. World hunger was my mother's weakness. She loved it. Because of her religious side. But that wasn't believable enough. She knew very well I've never been too hot for world hunger. I prefer tennis or reading. But it just so happened that for once we didn't have classes the next morning, which was Saturday. A teacher training day, they called it. That way, Friday evening became a part of the weekend, just this once. Of course that wasn't necessarily enough, with a mother like mine. My clever trick was to tell her that I'd gotten super-good grades in the last reporting period, which ended a few days earlier. That's what my mother cared about. It would be the perfect crime. The truth was, I'd gotten lousy grades, except in French. French is my best subject (as you're probably starting to realize). But my mother was really touched, because she suddenly felt I was making progress and everything. So she agreed to the Friday evening party thing. It killed me.

So I told everybody I was going. I even dared speak to Mathilde. She and I weren't in the same classes, except for German. *Ich liebe dich.* We saw each other twice a week. All during Tuesday's class that week I repeated the sentence in my head. "By the way, are you going to your sister's birthday party?" At the end of class I walked over, in spite of being scared, and asked her. She said, "Yes," with a little smile. And I almost died of a heart attack.

But my mother changed her mind. Over a truly trivial event, but which turned out badly. Marco and I got busted smoking in the bathroom between classes three days before the party. Really lousy luck. It wasn't anything real serious, if you want my opinion. Except that my mother really took it badly. She was always taking things that weren't important super badly. She said I was becoming a delinquent. No kidding. She said that. Whereas it was no problem that François, the guy she was living with, smoked more than a pack a day. I know, because the cigarettes I smoked were mainly the ones I swiped from his desk. Anyway, my mother wouldn't hear another word on that subject. Nothing. For her, smoking was like a crime. She was religious, I tell you. So things got hot. They even got super hot. Especially when she realized I'd been swiping my cigarettes from François. "He's paying your school tuition and this is how you thank him?" But he was such a loser, he even used a cigarette holder to smoke. Like in the days of the pyramids, or the Middle Ages. Just to remind you that he came from a noble family, in case you hadn't noticed. Pathetic, that's what I think it is.

Where I really was out of luck was that after the business with my cigarettes, the Institut principal gave me a warning, like the rules required, and my mother was called in on the very day of Emilie's party. I swear: the very same day. That turned into a super-hot scene. The three of us were in the boss-man's office. I won't describe the mood for you. I got shot down at point-blank range. And afterward my mother got angry, and she grounded me. As for going to Emilie Fermat's birthday, forget about it. I was in the wrong, I admit it. But honestly, I think it's unfair. It isn't right to go back on your decisions.

In reprisal I hung up a poster in my bedroom that I bought from a guy in the métro. It showed a man on a cross with his crown of thorns, and written underneath was, "He didn't smoke, he didn't drink, he didn't fuck. He died at thirty-three."

Chapter 3

When you think about it, Marco was really lucky, being able to do whatever he wanted. His parents must be really nice, for them to leave him alone in Paris. They must trust him, and all. Nice people always trust you; that's how you can tell they're nice. Still, I thought it was strange that parents would leave their son all alone in Paris, without worrying or anything. "What do your parents do, overseas?" I asked him, to clear up the mystery. He was barely listening to what I was saying. Too busy shining his shoes for Emilie Fermat's party. Marco was just the sort of guy to not answer you. You'd ask him a question and sometimes he'd answer, sometimes he wouldn't. You never knew. That kind of attitude has always made me crazy. If you ask me a question, I answer. Logical, right? But with him, no. He'd rather shine his shoes so you'd have to admit that they really looked sharp. "Not bad, huh?" He said that while looking at himself in the mirror, like he was talking to himself. I didn't answer. After all, I wasn't going to answer him when he'd been ignoring me. So I repeated my question: "Hey, why aren't your parents in Paris?" Marco went into the bathroom, still ignoring me because I hadn't answered him. That pissed me off, so I yelled, "Stop primping for a second! I'm asking you a question."

"They work. It's my father. He's with the phone company."

"Where?"

"I've already told you a thousand times."

"I forget."

"In Morocco."

Really, the guy was just too lucky. His parents had gone to Morocco six months earlier. Because they didn't want their son to wind up in some sort of international lycée there, and they thought the Institut was a good school, given its reputation, they'd left him behind in Paris, alone. And with a maid's room, to boot. The first time Marco told me that, it floored me. Really. Later, I found out things hadn't happened quite that way. That was Marco's personal version. His parents had actually entrusted him to his grandmother, who lived on the ground floor of the building but who also had this maid's room up on the top floor. The two of them had agreed that he could sleep up there. The rest of the time he was supposed to live with the old lady. But of course Marco didn't bother telling you that. He'd rather say that he lived alone. Like a college student, in other words.

"I'd really like it if my parents went to Morocco."

"What do your parents do?" he asked me as he came back into the room.

He had combed his hair back. I don't know what he put on his hair to make it stay like that. I tried it myself once. Not to copy him, but because I liked it. It didn't hold. I came home that evening with a kind of crest on top of my head, feeling totally embarrassed. But with Marco, it held. When he did that, he looked sort of Italian, like a Mafia guy and all. You could still see the comb marks.

"My father . . . It's complicated."

I didn't want to get into it. I never mentioned the fact that he was dead.

"What about your mother?"

"I don't really want to talk about my mother. She lives with this guy . . . No shit, the guy wears corduroy pants."

"Oh yeah. I get it."

"And the business about the warning really pissed him off. Sometimes I think it'd be best for me to get the hell out of there."

"Where would you go?"

"I don't know. Far away, I guess."

Marco was looking at me strangely. I still hadn't told him I wouldn't be able to come to the party after all, but I got the impression he suspected it. The fact was, I hadn't found a way to tell him without looking like a kid who'd been grounded by his mother. Marco had been busted for smoking too, of course. He probably got a warning, like me, but nobody cared, since no one was there to bawl him out (except his grandmother, who was probably asleep with her mouth open three quarters of the time). But I had to take the plunge sooner or later, so I just told

him I couldn't come. I had a better offer: a date with a girl
who was really hot and all. So of course I wasn't going to some
actress's party when I had a date the same evening. You'd have
to be stupid. Besides, what's the big deal with actresses,
anyway?

At first, he didn't believe me. He thought I was bullshitting
him. So I had to go into detail. Her name was Charlotte. She
was a brunette from my old school who smoked at least a pack
of cigarettes a day, and had dyed her hair red. The bit about the
red hair convinced him. You can't make something like that
up. That's my personal technique: drop some specific details right
in the middle of a huge lie. It muddies the waters.

In any case, I didn't mind bullshitting Marco, because I
knew very well that he often did the same thing. He was the
kind of guy to bullshit you from morning till night. To hear
him tell it, incredible things were always happening to him.
Compared to him, your life was really dullsville. I know guys
who would've taken all of it for the gospel truth. But with Marco
you couldn't ever take anything for the gospel truth, since he
made stuff up from morning 'til night. His problem was that he
didn't have a super-good memory. In fact, his memory was
totally shot. My own theory is that he drank too much. So what
happened was, he'd make up contradictory versions. If you ask
me, the guy lied all the time. Without even realizing it, sometimes. It was like a disease. Especially when it came to girls. He
told me things that were so amazing, I wound up not believing
anything. Even his story about Morocco was fishy, which is why

I kept bringing it up. It would be just like him to tell me that his father worked for the phone company in Tunisia or the Maghreb. I really would have liked to catch Marco in the act—red-tongued, so to speak. So I didn't mind bullshitting him from time to time. A fair swap, in a sense. Because of course I didn't have a date with Charlotte. It was just that I couldn't come, because of my mother.

"So why don't you bring her?"

"Who?"

"The girl you have a date with."

"Who's that?"

"The girl you have a date with."

"Huh?"

"The girl . . . "

"What girl?"

"The one you have a date with."

"Which one?"

By stringing him along like that, I was playing for time. Because I knew perfectly well what girl he was talking about. After all, there weren't ten thousand girls I could be dating. There was just one of them, plus I didn't have a date with her. But I wanted to confuse Marco a little, to give myself time to come up with a good excuse. What's annoying about people is that they always force you to make stuff up. You might feel like telling the truth, but they always manage to contradict you. No kidding, they always force you to make stuff up. Because they keep asking for explanations about everything. Only you can't explain everything all the time. If you tell them you can't go to a party, for example, right away they start asking for endless explanations, like for a medical certificate, instead of just understanding that you can't go. So you wind up simplifying things a little, you rearrange stuff, change things ever so slightly so you don't have to go into detail. It's just a little fiddling, but then they accuse you of lying. That's what's annoying about people. The lack of logic.

Why didn't I bring Charlotte to the party? I thought of telling him that it was because of money. Because maybe there'd be a cover charge, like super expensive. Just to get in. And then afterward there'd be drinks. It would wind up costing an arm and leg. Like I already said, at the Institut there were nothing but rich kids who got millions in pocket money every week. No kidding. And in dollars, too. But not me. So I couldn't go and pay two cover charges, mine and Charlotte's. It just wasn't within my means. Because, I may as well tell you, I was flat broke. I had spent everything I had.

Up to then I'd been staying afloat thanks to Madame Morozvitch. Denise Morozvitch. She was generous, at least. She used to pay me a little stipend every week. It was a secret. Especially from her, because she really wasn't aware of it. I didn't want to bother her; I preferred to just take it discreetly. Tactfully. But the scheme had fallen through. That had been a tough one to swallow. To tell you the whole story, Madame Morozvitch lived in the same building we did, one floor down. She was a nice little old lady, but really old, and she looked all banged up. You always felt she was going to die at any minute. And above all, she was blind. Or almost. Anyway, my mother looked after her. Ran errands for her, that sort of thing. The two of them got along great. Besides, my mother liked that, taking care of old ladies. It must have made her feel useful. Whatever. And since she thought my life lacked usefulness, she'd enlisted me in her project. Dragged me into it, actually. She decided I would visit Madame Morozvitch once a week, to look after her. A real horror show. Or at least it was a horror show in the beginning. I didn't know what to say to her. I didn't even know if she grasped who I was or what the heck I was doing in her living room. She'd slouch in her chair wearing her big dark glasses, and I'd just sit there feeling like a jerk, looking at her and not knowing what to do. It was torture. Sometimes I would tell her things, but her answers were way off base, or she didn't react at all. You could never tell if she was asleep, because of her glasses, or if she was about to croak. So I acted as if she was asleep. We got along better when we didn't talk, basically. We had more things to say to each other.

But after a while, the time started to hang heavy on my hands. Really. Two hours a week looking at yourself reflected in a pair of dark glasses can really bring you down. No kidding. So I decided to read stuff to her from the dusty-smelling books in her bookcase. I read them aloud. At the time, I didn't know I wanted to be a writer yet, considering that I didn't know a thing about books. And from then on, we got along pretty good, Madame Morozvitch and me. She was actually a lot less dead than I thought. She would sometimes come out with incredible things that would just floor you. I mean like about her life. She had lots of stories to tell. Unbelievable things. The rest of the time, I read to her.

Then one day she asked me to go get a letter she'd received that was in her desk. Because her son wrote to her from time to time. A real prick, from what I gathered, who dreamed of shipping her off to an old folks home so he could get his paws on the apartment. I swear. There are still people like that around. More and more of them, even. Anyway, I went to get the letter to read it to her, and as I was rummaging around, I found the stash where she hid her money: a wad of bills, like in the movies. I couldn't believe my eyes. I didn't touch anything then. But I thought about it all the next night. It's now or never, I told myself. After all, she was blind. I wouldn't risk a thing. Best to nibble a little at a time, I thought, so as not to get caught. Forewarned is forearmed. Maybe even five-armed, when you're dealing with a feebleminded old lady like Madame Morozvitch.

The following week, I didn't bother weighing the pros and cons. I pretended to step out for a moment and went into the next room, where she had what she called her "desk," which was actually a table with drawers. I didn't waste any time. In fact I really hurried. I took two twenty-euro bills. Now you see it, now you don't. Piece of cake! The easiest bank robbery in all of bank robbing history. High art, signed Julien Parme. But while my hand was still lingering lovingly in the drawer, I suddenly noticed Madame Morozvitch standing by the door a few feet away, looking at me. Yikes! I jumped like I'd never jumped in my life. There she was, hidden behind her dark glasses, not saying a word. What if she could see perfectly well? I suddenly wondered. You take an old lady who wears glasses, for example. Who's to say she's really blind? She might very well wear them so everybody would *think* she's blind, just to be cagey, and act accordingly. I gave her a tense smile and nervously stuffed the two bills in my pocket. I felt she was staring at me. I closed the drawer as quietly as I could, but she made a strange noise with her mouth, as if she knew. It scared the shit out of me. Damn. If my mother found out about this, I was screwed, let me tell you. I suggested to Madame Morozvitch that we go back to the living room. She gave a little smile like a witch, a knowing kind of smile, and I helped her back to her chair. Then I sat down, casual as hell. I cleared my throat, because for some reason my voice always chokes up a little when I'm uncomfortable, and also I scratch my nose when I'm nervous. They're just things I can't help doing. So I cleared my throat while scratching my nose and I started to read.

A moment later she interrupted me in the middle of a sentence: "You know, Julien, I want to say that it's very nice of you to come visit me like this."

I didn't know if she was referring to something, but I decided to act as if nothing was wrong.

"You're welcome, Madame Morozvitch. I'm glad to. It's nothing."

My voice was completely shot now, and if I kept scratching my nose I'd wind up looking like Michael Jackson.

"No, that's just the point; it's very nice of you. And that's why I'm touched."

Like I told you, she would sometimes come out with things that just floored you.

"We should all try to be a little more generous," I said evasively.

Then I started reading again, at top speed. She didn't say anything else that day. So I took that as consent. After all, it was better for her that I should be the one to take the money. Because if I hadn't taken it, it would've gone to her son. Eventually, I mean. And since the money was what the son was after, and that was why she and he didn't get along, it was better for everybody for me to take care of the money. It was a simple matter of logic. Always glad to do a favor. Because deep down, I liked Madame Morozvitch a lot. In fact, some day I'll give her back everything I took. I'll draw up accounts, and give everything back. I'll even add a little bit more, for interest. And I'll buy her flowers from time to time. It'll be with her money, of course, but that's not the point. The point is that she'll feel that people are looking after her. That people like her. That it smells nice in her room. Because if you want my opinion, it must be really depressing to be as old as she is. And blind, to boot. I'll bring her flowers and pastries. In that way, without her even being aware of it, at least the two of us would agree that it was a good idea for me to be stealing a little from her every week.

After my hour of reading that day, I felt super rich. I had forty euros in my pocket—international world class. Besides, I was going to be able to get more cash every week. I was only in high school, but I was already dreaming of getting a pension. I remember it very well: the weather was pretty warm, the first days of spring, and I felt crazy. I felt like going to sit on a café terrace and lazing in the sun. I walked over to Alésia, a neighborhood where I didn't know anybody. When the waiter came over, I said, "A whiskey, please!" trying to sound like a writer at the peak of his fame. He hesitated for a moment, because of the hour and maybe also because of my age. I thought he was going to say no. But he didn't say anything, which must mean yes in waiter language, right? I'll leave him a huge tip for his trouble, I told myself. I've always dreamed of leaving huge tips. To see the guy's reaction. The waiter suddenly realizes that he's dealing with Julien Parme. He can't believe his eyes. And I'm getting up, about to leave, I'm a few feet away when you see him racing after me, "Monsieur, monsieur!" all out of breath, sweating, and emotional, really emotional, blown away, it's the chance of a lifetime. He hands me a copy of my latest novel and asks if I would be kind enough and with warmest regards to dedicate the masterpiece . . . Yeah, I remember, I felt really rich that day, with forty euros in my pocket. Everything seemed possible, even becoming a great writer. I also remember that I bought a pack of cigarettes and spent the whole afternoon smoking in the sun, dreaming about all the novels I'd write. I felt good. No worries. With the incredible feeling of being free and having all of life in front of me.

Especially since it hardly made any difference to Madame Morozvitch. She could afford it. On the other hand, it let me finance smokes, movies, books, and lots of other stuff. And it was an extra reason to come see her every Saturday. In the end, even though I'm not a thief, at least not in my soul, I didn't feel any shame, except the ongoing shame of not feeling any. I usually hit her up for twenty euros. Rarely more. In the beginning I wrote everything down, compulsive accounting, but I quit because I always messed it up. I've never been real sharp with numbers. But when the time comes when I can pay, it'll be easy to find out how much I owe her. A nice tidy sum, when you think of it. To be deducted from my royalties. In fact, I'll have to mention it to my publisher. When I have one. When I write a book.

Anyway, the problem was that one day her son just shipped her off to a nursing home. Even though she was still in great shape. What he wanted was the apartment. I don't mean to brag, but here's the proof that I was right about that: he moved into the apartment a month later. It made me sick. I'm sure he didn't bother asking his mother what she thought. That sort of stuff depresses you for a month. Especially because I lost a fair amount of money in the process, since the desk was still pretty full. But I wasn't about to come read to that asshole just so I could go on helping myself. That was out of the question. I'm not in the habit of reading to assholes. I have principles, after all.

Chapter 4

Maybe that's what I should've told Marco: that I couldn't go because of the money. It was a way of lying while telling the truth. But I wound up thinking that it was a bad idea. I couldn't imagine that girl (I mean Emilie Fermat) making us pay a cover charge. If it had been in a nightclub, okay, but in her house, and for her birthday—it wasn't very likely. It would look like an excuse. And then I would've had to tell Marco the truth, namely that I was going to miss out on the party of the year because of my mother. It was enough to make you sick.

So as not to have to answer Marco right away, I lit myself a cigarette. That's what I like best about smoking: lighting up. That's what does it for me. I always scrunch my eyebrows in a frown when I light a cigarette. No special reason. Some things just can't be explained. You'd have to explain it to the people who think that everything can be explained.

"You have one for me?"

Marco was still looking at himself in the mirror. Bare chested and all. If he could have kissed himself, he'd have done

JULIEN PARME · 33

it. I swear. It's crazy how the guy could be in love with himself. So much the better for him, but still. Though you had to admit that he did pretty well for himself. Just looking at Marco, you understood right away why girls went for him. His age probably had a lot to do with it, and he had a good build. He put on a white shirt, a really plain one, along the lines of, hey, check out my style. Then he turned to take the cigarette I was holding out to him, and asked like for the fourth time: "So why don't you bring her along, the girl you have the date with?"

"She isn't into that kind of party," I finally answered.

"Oh, yeah? What kind is she into?"

Marco always had to have the last word. People who always want to have the last word get on my nerves. Because there is no last word. Never. There's always another one that slips in right behind. That's just the way it is. He should know that. First of all, how was I supposed to know what kind of party Charlotte was into, seeing as I'd never even met this Charlotte? Marco had brought me down with his endless preparations and his thousands of questions. I felt like going home. Damn. I can't wait to be eighteen. Freedom. Because now, I sort of feel like a dog chained to a post, with a rope chafing my neck. I'm always reminded that I'm in jail when grown-ups say, "When you're eighteen, you can do whatever you like."

I was scratching little lines on the walls of my cell.

Marco turned to me. He was finally ready. "What do you think?" he asked. "You forgot to put on lipstick," I said, to show him I actually wasn't as tense as I looked. "Don't worry about that," he shot back. "I'll have some on me pretty soon, and not just on my lips." The allusion pissed me off. It's exactly what I was telling you earlier: he was showing off, pure and simple. Then he told me he had to hurry because he was expecting a girl to come pick him up before they went to the party. The business about the girl coming to get him didn't surprise me. I'm even sure he always had them do that. Really, the guy was too much of a show-off. It was to let her know that he had a maid's room of his own. He was showing his cards, in a way. For after the party.

"So who's the girl?"

"You'd like to know, wouldn't you?"

"Nah, I don't care."

I pretended to be looking for something in my pockets.

"Her name's Charlotte, too," he said. "Funny, huh?"

I wondered if he was putting me on. Marco was exactly the kind of guy to tell you something like that, to make fun of you. The guy had no finesse. I clicked my tongue. I don't know why. Sometimes I do things without knowing why. It was probably to show that I wasn't rattled. If he didn't believe my Charlotte story, too bad for him. I wasn't about to beg or anything. I got up from the armchair. My legs were stiff. "All right. I'm going." I was already late, but I honestly didn't feel like going home. After what had happened in the principal's office . . . Marco turned to me with an odd smile, and said:

"So who do you think this girl is?"

"No idea."

"It's Mathilde."

I practically choked.

"Who? Mathilde Fermat?"

"Yeah."

Damn . . . It took me at least ten seconds to realize what he had just laid on me. What? Mathilde Fermat, who was practically my fiancée? I could have crumpled to the ground. It was the worst news of the day. Of the year, even. Just then Marco's cell phone rang. He went into the kitchen to answer it, so I wouldn't hear, I suppose. Mathilde Fermat? I slapped my forehead. I couldn't believe it. What the hell was she doing with a guy like Marco? Life doesn't make any sense. What could she see in a guy like him, someone so dense and all? Nothing made any sense anymore. Marco came back into the living room, which was also his bedroom.

"Okay, I have to get cracking. She'll be here soon."

She'd called to warn him that she'd be a bit early, so he was speeding up. He started putting away the clothes strewn on the bed and armchair. Everything was happening too fast for me.

"I can't believe it."

"What?"

"Did you tell her that I was at your place?"

"Tell who?"

"Mathilde."

"I don't remember. Damn, look how you wrinkled it. You really are a jerk."

It's true, I hadn't noticed the shirt. But what was he thinking, putting it on a chair? After all, chairs are for sitting, so you shouldn't be surprised if a shirt on a chair gets all wrinkled. It's a matter of logic, pure and simple. But logic was something Marco had never heard of.

"How soon will she be here?"

"Right away. She called to say she was coming. She wanted the door code."

She was on her way. Damn. She wanted the code. I didn't understand anything anymore. I didn't know the two of them even knew each other, since Marco took Spanish, not German.

"Where'd you know her from, huh? I didn't know you knew each other."

I'd never seen them together or anything. And I'd never dared tell Marco what I felt for Mathilde. Never dared tell him that I thought about her and her pretty mouth every night before going to sleep, that she was the person I liked most in the world, and that I'd almost passed out cold the other day, when I spoke to her. No kidding. Out cold. From the emotion and all. And here he was, telling me I was about to run into her here. Without any preparation. Here he was, folding his undershirt as carefully as a girl, and I was maybe about to see Mathilde Fermat. Damn. We really weren't on the same wavelength, him and me.

"And then you're going straight to the party?"

"Well, yeah."

"Then why is she coming to your place when the party's at her house?"

Marco was making his bed now. And I suddenly realized that pig might be bringing Mathilde back here, after the party. I don't know why, but the idea struck me as horrible. Absolutely horrible, even. And I also remembered what he'd said about lipstick. The bastard. He was talking about her when he told me he'd have lipstick all over himself. I wondered if Mathilde Fermat was the kind of girl who wore lipstick. Probably yes, to go to a party. "But why's she coming to your place?" Marco had opened the window to let in some fresh air. He inspected himself in the mirror one last time. Then he said: "You ready?"

On the edge of panic, I started searching my pockets. I pulled out a cigarette and lit it, frowning. Only this time, I knew why I was frowning.

"Damn, that's really something. And she's coming here?"

"I told you, she'll be here any minute."

Maybe I would run into her on the stairs. I felt majorly stressed. I wondered if I would dare speak to her. If I'd known, I would've worn my black jacket, the one I love. Because I really wasn't ready. I was being taken by surprise. I started to get panicky. Mathilde Fermat. What if she asked me why I wasn't coming to her sister's party? I'd have to make something else up to tell Marco. It would be just like him to say that my mother was punishing me. A traitor, that's what he was. Now he wanted to put on some music and was searching everywhere for a CD. I heard him muttering that he couldn't find the CD he was looking for. I asked him again how it had happened, and why she was coming to his place, and what for. He was vague. His mind was on his stereo. He wanted to set the mood. Damn. Why wasn't I going to that party? I felt disgusted. But mainly, I wanted to become invisible.

"All right. I'm going. Give her my regards."

"No problem."

"And if she asks why I'm not coming . . ."

"Right. Don't sweat it."

"Thanks. Okay, so long."

"So long."

I left the bedroom. Just as I was closing the door behind me, I heard his stupid voice saying, "And good luck with your Charlotte!" Marco could really be a major asshole. He was just the kind of guy to wish you luck with your Charlotte while knowing perfectly well that you were going to spend the evening alone. I pressed the elevator button. I wanted to get out of there. Because I was afraid I wouldn't have anything to say to Mathilde, and she'd think I was ridiculous. In the darkness, the elevator light blinked for ages. I was more nervous than I've ever been. Mathilde Fermat. In the distance I heard music. I realized that Marco had found his CD. What a jerk he was! Then the elevator came. And I plunged all the way down in the darkness, trembling like a creature on the run.

Chapter 5

When I say, "I plunged all the way down in the darkness," I'm sure some smart ass will tell me that's not the way you say it. So I'll say right away that I'm well aware of that. What makes me crazy is when people sarcastically shoot you down for using a figure of speech. So if you say, "I plunged down," some guy will ironically say, "Oh, so you didn't plunge up?" Well, nine times out of ten I feel like killing them. I think that sort of snappy little remark is just plain stupid. Because if you ask me, when someone says "plunging down," they're saying something specific. And if somebody tries to make fun of me for saying that, I tell them right away that you can very well plunge up or climb down, but it's very hard to do because you have to have a feeling for poetry, and not everybody has that, especially not idiots who think they speak better French than other people.

I walked home without seeing anything around me, I was thinking about Mathilde so hard. I usually never take the elevator to go upstairs. A matter of principle. Elevators are for old people and Eskimos. That's why I always take the stairs, and I usually run up them. First, because I'm always in a rush, like all great writers. But mainly it's a reflex. It's my legs, they just go crazy at the first step. Don't ask me why; I have no idea. It's just that when I see a flight of stairs, I start to run. I can't help it. As a result, I was out of breath as usual when I got to the door to our apartment on the top floor. I felt like puking. Everything made me feel like puking, if you want the details. The floors I just climbed, the fake marble of the stairwell, the door in front of me, what was behind it—I mean my mother and all. Total disgust. I imagined turning around and leaving. I didn't know where. Just leaving. Saying to hell with all of them. And then going to the party, finding Mathilde, and telling her I loved her. Just living. If life were a novel, that's what I'd do, I told myself. That's what I'd do if I had the guts. Life is a novel when you have guts. Hot damn, an aphorism! Oh man! The lines I come up with sometimes! I quickly grabbed a pencil from my bag, sat down on the top step, and wrote it down so I wouldn't forget it. I circled it twice, and wrote, "For the novel" next to it. I don't mean to brag, but I have lines like that scattered all through my things. When I recopy them all one day, it'll make a real novel, I swear. And on Page 1 you'll see: "For Mathilde, who inspired me."

I spent a long time sitting on the top step of the stairs. The timer clicked off the light automatically, and I sat in the darkness without moving, daydreaming. I also felt like having a cigarette, but on the family landing, that was a little risky. Especially since I'd led my mother to think I was going to quit.

But the urge was too strong, so I went down a few steps and opened a little window and lit myself a cigarette, frowning. Like in the movies. Yeah, leave. That would be classy. Go to Italy, say. I'd seen photos of Italy, it was the most beautiful country in the world. The land of tiramisu. I'd be able to manage just fine there. I'd work to earn some money, enough to stay at a little seaside hotel, and life would be great. In the evenings I'd go to bars to pick up girls. I'd tell them about my adventures. Well, I might add a little about my reasons for leaving. Hardly anything. Just a little murder here and there. To make it sexier. And they'd fall in love with me. Then I'd write a letter to the Institut. I could already see their faces. They'd be jealous as hell. And another letter to Madame Thomas, explaining why I couldn't ask her to come join me, in spite of the literary and reciprocal desire, because I would be marrying Mathilde soon.

I sighed deeply. On the other side of the door, I heard the phone ring, then my mother's voice. It must've been at least nine o'clock. I was going to catch hell for sure. Especially since I didn't have an excuse or anything. Oddly enough, though, I took my time. I chewed a mint tic tac for my breath. It occurred to me that Mathilde must be in that bastard Marco's bedroom right about then. I could imagine him giving her something to drink. Like wine, making a big show of it. Or worse, a Coke with an aspirin in it. I've heard it really turns girls on for sex. An afuckodisiac, in other words. Frankly, it made me sick.

I went to the window again to toss the cigarette butt away. You always have to get rid of the evidence. Walking into the apartment with a butt in your pocket would be like killing a guy and keeping the gun on you when you went through customs. I'm not that crazy. I leaned out to watch the butt fall, and followed it with my eyes as long as I could. It suddenly vanished, like magic. A disappearance. I imagined a body falling. I imagined that I was the body. It sent a chill down my spine. I closed the window to think about something else.

I climbed back up to the landing. I took out my keys and, just as I was about to put them in the lock, the door opened. It was Bénédicte; she'd probably heard me. I bet she was on the lookout for me coming home. That would be like her, anyway.

"Oh, there you are. They've been looking for you everywhere. You're gonna get chewed out. I wouldn't want to be in your shoes."

She said that in her sanctimonious little simper. It really pissed me off. I stood there a moment longer, as if paralyzed. I could hear a voice inside me saying: "Leave! Go as far away as you can! Beat it! Nobody in this dump is on your side! Get out while you still have time. Be brave!" I looked out the stairwell window. Outside, it was night. It was late. I took a deep breath to calm myself. There would always be time enough to leave later. And I walked into the apartment like a good boy.

I realize that I haven't told you about Bénédicte yet. She's François the Particule's daughter. Sort of my stepsister, if you like. What's funny, though, is that she looks a lot like my mother.

Her face, I mean. Even though they don't have any connection at the biological level. Everyone says they look like each other, as if my mother were actually her mother. Which isn't the case, since she's my mother. Every time somebody says that, the two of them look happy. They take it as a compliment, whereas most of the time it's just a passing remark. François also likes the idea that his wife and his daughter sort of look like each other. I'm the only one who finds it completely uninteresting. Just so long as nobody says I look like François.

He and my mother had started living together almost two years earlier. I must have been around twelve, almost thirteen. One day we changed apartments and came to live here, with them. Before that, the place where my mother and I lived was kind of small, but I liked it. Whereas this place was a huge apartment in the Trocadéro neighborhood with a view of the Eiffel Tower. No kidding. That's when I first met Bénédicte. At first, I thought she was really good looking. She had long, very straight blonde hair that came almost down to her ass. But she and I never got along. In fact, we've never done anything except fight. She's two years older than me. The same age as Marco. They ran into each other once. He had come to get something at my place. We were in my room, and Bénédicte walked in without knocking, as usual. Afterward Marco talked to me about her. He thought she was great looking, and seriously stacked, in his opinion. Maybe, but she was really a jerk. She went horseback riding every weekend, for example. Girls who are crazy about horses are always uptight and hard to get along with. That's a rule. Take a girl who goes riding every week, and she'll be totally immature about life. The kind who says she's not interested in boys. A little girl forever telling other people how to behave. A quibbler. Always saying her prayers, straightening things, or doing her homework. Frankly, girls like that are everything I hate. Especially since girls like that usually hate boys like me. Poets, I mean.

The truth is, Bénédicte was bored with life, but she was too proud to admit it. She'd never dare say something like that. She was always in her room studying, for example. And if you asked her why she hadn't finished yet, considering that she'd already been working for hours, she'd answer that she was getting ahead on her homework. That means doing work that isn't due the next day, but for the days after. So of course she was bored. Getting ahead on your homework is what people who are bored think to do. And when you're bored, you're the kind of person who spies on other people's lives, on people who are alive. You stand right by the door, so you can be the first person to pounce on them when they come in and to tell them in a snippy tone: "You're gonna get bawled out. I wouldn't want to be in your shoes."

That's what I mean.

I made a beeline for my room to drop off my things. Dinner was usually in the kitchen, in other words at the other end of the apartment. I went into the bathroom to splash some water on my face, and also to brush my teeth. You can't always trust tic tacs. And when you're dealing with my mother, better safe than sorry. Given the situation, I should have hurried and gone to see them. But for some reason I wasn't afraid of my mother's reaction that day. It was different. I took my time. I was too upset about the business with Mathilde. I didn't give a damn about the rest. They could yell at me as much as they liked. Suddenly I had an idea: to phone Marco's grandmother, make her think that I was with him up in his room. I would say that she absolutely had to come up to see him right away, because he wasn't feeling well and had barfed everywhere. Of course he would have told Mathilde that he lived alone, like a college student, and that his parents were abroad, all for show. So right in the middle of his routine, his grandmother would have walked in carrying stuff for an upset stomach. I loved the idea. Ha, ha! But I heard reproachful heels clicking down the hallway, and I zipped back to my bedroom without having time to carry out my plan.

My mother came in right behind me. "Do you realize what time it is?" She was looking at me with very hard eyes. Harder than stone, even. Like her heart.

I always felt my mother didn't really love me. I think she had a very definite idea of what a son should be, and that I was the opposite of that idea. I could clearly visualize the son she would've wanted to have. If I just closed my eyes, I could see him standing in front of me. He'd be looking down at me, with an ironic, scornful little smile that meant, "You'll never measure up, buddy. I'm the one she loves." He was blond, like her, and a good student, polite and well spoken. He wanted to be an engineer later on, and he'd love model airplanes, for example.

Every year on his birthday my mother would buy him a new kit. There was nothing to it. You always knew what to get him, and each time he was super happy and kept saying thank you. Whereas the year before, I'd made a face when she gave me a kind of thing in pieces that you had to glue together and paint, and you wound up with a crappy-looking airplane. A really great present. I told her I wasn't ten years old anymore, and that a scale model wasn't exactly what a man dreams of getting. But she refused to recognize that I wasn't a child anymore. Whereas the other one, the blond, always said thank you. And he'd skip a grade nearly every year because he got ahead on his homework in the evening after school, instead of hanging out with pals and smoking, like me. At convocation, he was always at the top of the honor roll. In short, the guy was perfect. I could see all that in her eyes. And it chilled me.

"I'm speaking to you. Do you realize what time it is?" "Yes," I said. She seemed outraged by my answer. As if I was trying to get her goat. Me, if you ask me a question, I answer. That's all. I wasn't about to say, "No," since she knew perfectly well when I'd come home, after all. What a dumb idea, to ask questions when you already know the answer and you know it'll make you angry. Only a mother would do that. Did I already tell you that mothers are all out of their minds? But I could see that things might take a turn for the worse. So I tried to come up with an excuse at top speed. Why was I coming home so late? I took a quick glance at the clock above my desk. It was past eight thirty. That would be hard to explain, considering that we got out of class around six. But I could always feed her some huge line of bullshit. Just then I saw Bénédicte's face appear at my door. That little hypocrite didn't want to miss a moment of my being chewed out. She was a scale model of a stepdaughter. My mother adored her. And she especially adored adoring her. It made one big blended family where everybody loved each other very much. I was the only blemish. I was the only problem in their life, actually.

At that moment, I realized it was true: the two of them really did look a lot like each other. What they lacked was a heart. One thought led to another, and I suddenly felt fed up. All at once, just like that, I let it all out. I said: "I know, it's late. So what? I was with Marco. We were talking. I didn't notice the time. It's no big deal." My mother didn't like it when you talked to her like that. She was the one who decided what was a big deal. Her, and not you. Especially given the lousy situation I was in.

"What do you mean it's no big deal? I've been waiting for you for two hours, Julien," my mother yelled furiously. "It's nearly nine o'clock. That's no time to be coming home! Do you hear? And the same week you got a warning, too!"

I shrugged my shoulders, because I didn't know what to say. She looked at me in despair, as if the mere fact of my existence drove her to her wits' end. "What have I done to deserve such a son? I mean, what have I done?" That was typical of what she said when she wanted to make me feel that she couldn't stand me anymore. She would say things like that while looking up at the ceiling instead of at me, that is, up to God who according to her was just on the other side, like on a seventh floor. But God didn't answer her. He left her all alone with her dumb question. What had she done to have a son like me? If she just put her mind to it a little, she'd be sure to remember what she'd done to have me. Considering that to have a son there aren't a million ways of going about it. I have my own idea about that, and the angrier she got, the more trouble I had imagining that she once could have been that sweet young woman in a bed with my father, like two lovers doing dirty stuff, like Mathilde and me, for example. Except that for the moment the thing my mother had done to have me was what that asshole Marco would be enjoying with Mathilde, and that was making me crazy. My mother was bawling me out, but I didn't give a damn. My heart was someplace else. Everything she said just bounced right off. All I could think of was the fact that Marco was making it with Mathilde. With nocturnal allusions and all. Suddenly it made me super angry. My mother did nothing but scream, and that's when I sort of lost it.

"Why are you always yelling?" I asked her.

"I beg your pardon?"

"You must enjoy it, screaming your head off. I don't know, can't you talk calmly?"

"Don't you use that tone of voice with me, Julien. You change that tone immediately!"

"But you're the one who's always screaming! And if you want my opinion, that's not very smart. Yeah. It's not too smart to talk to me that way. Because remember, I'll be choosing your nursing home in a few years."

She changed color before my eyes. I knew I'd gone too far. But I was feeling too desperate that evening. It's true. I was out of control. I couldn't help myself. Just then, I heard François's malignant voice calling to my mother. It was like the bell in a boxing match. It was time, he said. Time for what? That's when I realized that she was all dressed up. They probably had a dinner or something to go to.

"Are you making fun of me? How dare you speak to me like that? Do you even realize what the situation is?"

"Catherine!"

It was the Particule again. He always worried about being late. My mother paused for a moment before continuing. "All right. You're in luck, I don't have time now. I have to leave. But we'll talk about this tomorrow. Believe me, Julien, you and I are going to have a little talk. We have a lot to talk about. I'll see you tomorrow." She spun on her heel. You'd have thought we were in a bad movie. With a bad actress who wanted you to understand that she was supposed to be real angry just then. Before going out the door, my mother stopped in her tracks, like she was struck by lightning. She looked at me as if she was about to tell me something important—really important, even. She opened her mouth, but finally didn't say anything. Weird. After which she left my room, immediately followed by Bénédicte. "Good riddance," I said, once they were at the other end of the hallway and couldn't hear me anymore. With women, it's simple: you either love them or hate them. With those two, it wasn't much of a choice.

I heard the front door slam. It echoed in my head. A truce. I took a deep breath and stretched out on my bed. What had I done to deserve a mother like that? That was the real question. Because honestly, it wasn't like I'd killed somebody. The only explanation for all this was that I was in love. That's all. But my mother couldn't understand. Since she didn't have a heart, and "being in love" no longer meant anything to her since my father's death.

I closed my eyes and thought of him. I told myself that nothing like this would have happened if he hadn't abandoned us. It's true. And I started talking to him, the way I sometimes do. I know, it's stupid to talk to a dead person, but I've always done it. Bénédicte makes fun of me because she thinks I'm talking to myself. She says I'm crazy. But go try to explain to her that I'm talking to my father, and that it's the only way I've found not to feel too sad. Try to explain that to a girl who goes horseback riding every week.

Chapter 6

Bénédicte was fooling around in her room. I could hear her pacing on the other side of the wall. I felt like she was on the lookout, but for what? For the chance to come give me a hard time, probably. It was too bad, because I would have loved to have a really nice sister, someone I could talk to about everything. But Bénédicte was so totally frustrated that you couldn't talk to her about anything. Unless it was about horses. But I didn't want to do that, on principle. Especially since I knew her routine by heart. Every Saturday she went to her club outside of Paris, near some forest or other. Sometimes she rode in competitions. In the beginning, I used to go watch. Her riding helmet and crop made me laugh. If I rode horses, I'd wear a different kind of outfit. A riding helmet and crop is really pathetic. If you ask me, the only way to ride a horse is like in the movies, with a cowboy hat. Otherwise you really look lame. It's a little like skiing with a wool bonnet. It's too hokey, if you know what I mean. I could imagine myself riding up to the lycée on my horse, with a cowboy hat and everything. I would sweep Mathilde up.

Tell her that we weren't going to spend our whole life in this miserable dump. That it was time to leave. To go far, far away. Beyond the desert. My horse would rear up, and the adventure would begin. Yeah. And Marco would be stuck there like an idiot, watching us ride off into the sunset.

Bénédicte was about seventeen. I imagined suggesting that she come to Emilie Fermat's party with me, without telling the parents. That would have blown her away, the little goody-goody. The idea was ridiculous, of course, because if I ever asked Bénédicte to a party, she would refuse without even thinking about it. Just on principle, the principle being that everything that comes from me disgusts her. No kidding. She says so all the time. Just because we share the same bathroom and she claims I spend ages in the shower. (It's not my fault I like to be clean.) And also because I once tried to drown her cat. That turned out to be a big deal. The cat's name was Kitty—no kidding. That Bénédicte would call her cat Kitty should tell you a lot about her personality. Only a girl who was completely clueless would do that. A girl who could think straight would call it something else. But Kitty, that's really pathetic. I never got along with that cat. He was forever underfoot, spying on what I was doing, leaving tons of hairs on my bed. In a word, the cat bugged me. But he was Bénédicte's best friend. He'd start to purr as soon as she came within a yard of him and would rub up against her every which way. For an animal, I think that's gross. So one day I tried a little experiment. I had run a bath. (As a rule I tend to take showers. But I had run myself a bath, don't ask me why.)

Kitty was prowling around. And because Bénédicte had snitched on me to the parents because I had supposedly stolen some money from the dresser, I decided to take revenge. Especially since my mother had been really harsh, yelling at me before she even considered whether I'd really done it. Unbelievable! No presumption of innocence in this dump! Under the circumstances, I decided to give them their money back right away. Needless to say, the shit hit the fan. So Bénédicte deserved a little symbolic punishment, and that's how I got the idea of running a bath and tossing Kitty in the water.

With an Olympic effort, he managed to climb out of the tub, but he didn't look so hot anymore. He was hugging the walls, dripping water everywhere. I really got a kick out of it. But then I took pity on him, wanted to fluff him up with the hair dryer, but he was being standoffish, so I left him alone. When Bénédicte found out what I had done, she went out of her gourd. And then two days later, the cat died of a heart attack. I swear. Just like that. He was lying there, and bang! he died. I honestly don't think it had any connection with the bath I'd made him take. But Bénédicte was sure it did. She thought I had deliberately traumatized him to the point of giving him a heart attack. She called me a killer. From then on, she started to hate me. Even though the veterinarian explained to her that it wasn't my fault. The cat had a heart murmur. But she wasn't buying it. She hung a framed photo of Kitty in her bedroom, next to her thousands of horse posters. She would pray in front of it at night, before going to sleep. No kidding.

I opened my bedroom door again. Not a sound in the whole apartment. The coast was clear. I went into the kitchen to make myself some dinner. When the parents were out, I usually made up a tray and ate in my room or else in front of the TV. The problem with the TV is that Bénédicte would show up within three minutes to criticize whatever program I chose and make my life miserable, so I preferred my bedroom. Before I opened the fridge, I absentmindedly turned on the kitchen radio. I roamed the dial for a moment until I came across a song that was really beautiful, but heartbreakingly sad. I stood listening to it without knowing what it was. It killed me. I had tears in my eyes. I couldn't understand the lyrics because it was badly pronounced English, but I was positive that it spoke to what I felt in my heart. After the shitty day I'd had. And then what I really wanted was a cigarette. I wanted to be far away and to smoke a cigarette. I don't know if you've noticed, but sadness always makes you want to be far away and smoking cigarettes. And if you're a writer, it also makes you want to write.

When the song ended, I took a stray piece of paper and a pencil. I closed my eyes (my technique to make inspiration come). What could I write? A poem, I thought at first. A poem for Mathilde, say. That was a good idea. I opened my eyes to get started, but nothing came. I lacked concentration, and I was all twisted over the kitchen counter. So I sat down, put the sheet of paper squarely in front of me, cleared my throat, and closed my eyes again. Maximum concentration. I tried to imagine powerful things. Mathilde, for example. I was already feeling moved, just by the idea that I was going to write my first real poem, which would go down in history. Something really impressive, with rhymes and all. I opened my eyes again. I was sure inspiration would come, but I was thirsty. I stood up and went to drink from the faucet. I looked out the kitchen window to the courtyard. When you leaned out you could sometimes see inside the apartment opposite. I always thought I would catch sight of a naked woman walking in front of her window. I went to sit back down and spent a long time in front of the sheet of paper, thinking about the publication of my collected works. I could already see myself in a black-and-white photo on the back cover, looking in despair and smoking a cigarette. Or a cigar, I couldn't decide. We'd see. I would send the collection to Madame Thomas. And to all the girls who had ignored me. They would kick themselves, the little bitches. They'd passed up their chance to inspire one of the greatest writers of the century. Too bad for them. It was too late. They would beg me to come back, but I would be like a stone, in spite of their physical allusions.

I tore up the blank sheet in front of me and took another one, then went to drink from the faucet before sitting down again. I was ready. To work! But nothing came. So I again applied my good old technique of closing my eyes. And clenched my teeth this time. To force the ideas to come. I opened my eyes again. Still nothing. Strange. This wasn't the right place to write. A kitchen has never produced masterpieces, it's a known fact. So I opened a couple of cupboards and took out a box of cookies. My dinner. Along with one of the bottles of wine lying around. All great writers are alcoholics. That's a known fact, too. I slipped it under my shirt, in case I ran into Bénédicte. I took the corkscrew from the drawer, stuffed it in my pocket, and left the kitchen. No need for a glass, I would drink straight from the bottle, like Balzac and the others. After all, this was the ideal evening to start my great novel. Yeah, all things considered, a novel was more appropriate than a poem. I would write about everything: the party I couldn't go to, the loneliness of my bedroom, the Eiffel Tower lighting up the living room, my mother in the principal's office, my wanting to weep in Mathilde's arms—everything that was in my heart. In short, a classic. I tiptoed the length of the apartment and was within a few feet of my room when I heard Bénédicte behind me.

"What are you doing?"

I stopped dead.

"Huh?"

"What are you doing?"

"Nothing. Forget it."

"Do you think I didn't see you?"

"If you're referring to the bottle under my shirt, I really don't know what you're talking about."

She didn't say anything, which gave me time to go into my room and lock the door behind me. No peace and quiet to write novels in this place! I put all my writing materials on my desk and opened the window. I started by wondering what to call my book. Personally, I think a big novel should have a big

title. Because a big novel with a small title seems cramped
and falsely humble. And a little novel with a big title is really
pretentious—like I'm the only person not to notice that I write
like shit. The other solution is to write a small novel with a small
title, but in that case you may as well stay home. No, there's
only one solution for writers like me, I mean the great ones,
and that's a killer title. Along the lines of *Journey to the End of the
Night*, but that one's already taken; I checked. Suddenly someone knocked on my door. It was Bénédicte. So I said:

"Who is it?"

"Who do you think?"

"What do you want?"

"I have to talk to you."

I hesitated for a moment.

"I'm working."

"What at?"

"I'm getting ahead on my homework."

Obviously, she didn't believe me.

"Listen . . ."

"What is it now?"

"Open up!"

"When your name is Bénédicte, you keep quiet," I
answered.

It's true, who would ever choose a name like Bénédicte?

"If you were in my place . . ."

"If I were in your place, honestly, I would have left long
ago."

Bam! A clean shot, right between the eyes! This time she didn't know what to say. In fact she was silent for a long time, but I knew very well that she was still standing on the other side of the door. I ignored her. I wondered what Bénédicte did in life before meeting me. What did she waste her time on? Who did she bug, to unwind? Now, because of her and her presence behind the door, I had lost my train of thought. Oh yes, the title. To get inspired, I took out the corkscrew. Then Bénédicte said:

"You absolutely mustn't open that bottle you took."

"What bottle?"

Just then, the cork popped.

"It's for the parents, Julien. They have to sample it first! What in the world are you doing? Wait! It's for the wedding. Do you hear me?"

I almost choked in the middle of a huge swallow. In fact, I spit it out onto the carpet. What wedding? I opened the door. Her face looked like a bad dream.

"What wedding?"

"Whose do you think?"

She sprinted to her room. Damn. Going riding every Saturday had really made her stupid. I followed her to her room.

"Bénédicte!"

I had taken the bait, but I still wanted to know. She tried to close her door, but I blocked it with my foot. I had no trouble opening it all the way; I'm stronger than she is. She was wearing a radiant smile. Illuminated with perversity. She made me sick.

"What are you talking about?"

"Nothing."

She was really treating me like an idiot. I jumped on her to strangle her. I tightened my hands around her neck with all my might. She started screaming and making strange noises. You would've thought it was a cow having its throat cut. Or a nanny goat; it was higher pitched. Then I let her go.

"You're completely nuts, you loser! You're just like your father! Completely wacko! You should be committed! That's what should happen to you! Be put away, like your father!"

There it was again. The usual song and dance.

"Whose wedding, Bénédicte?"

"Shut up."

"Answer me or I'll do it again!"

I came closer, intending to wring her neck. She responded by slapping me. Pow! A real sharp one, that cracked in the air. That's when I understood what she was trying to tell me. Suddenly I had trouble breathing. I swear. I felt sick. I sat down on her bed. My eyes were stinging, burning even. Bénédicte was scared. She sat down next to me and asked me about seventy-nine times if I was okay. She must've felt guilty about slapping me. Then she tried to comfort me. But I wasn't moving anymore. She was jumping all around, as if in a panic. Talking at top speed. A lunatic. But I was barely listening to what she was running on about, like she'd made a mistake, that was why she'd run away so fast, that she felt bad, that she had supposedly forgotten that I didn't know about the wedding business, that it just came out because of the bottle of wine.

"Liar," I finally said. "You knew perfectly well I didn't know. That's just why you told me. To be mean."

"Of course not. I forgot."

"I know that you knew."

"That I knew what?"

"That I didn't know."

"I didn't, I swear."

"How long have you known about their getting married?"

"I don't know. Two, maybe three days, that's all. I overheard a conversation, so afterward, that's when they told me. I'm sure they were certainly going to tell you, too."

"So why haven't they told me yet?"

"They were going to tell you, like I said, but considering the way you are—really unpredictable and touchy. I suppose they wanted to pick a good time."

A good time. What a bunch of damned traitors! My mother must have been afraid to tell me because she knew very well that I hated François, the larger-than-life asshole. That's probably why she had been nicer these last few days. Why she'd at first agreed to let me go to Emilie Fermat's party, for example. Yeah. I suddenly realized that she had been laying the groundwork for at least ten days. Before I got busted for smoking between classes. I felt sick.

I stood up.

"Where are you going?"

I had tears in my eyes now. I especially didn't want Bénédicte to see me like that. If I bawled like a girl in front of her, I'd never hear the end of it. Particularly since it wasn't because I was sad that I had tears in my eyes. It was just that my eyes were stinging, and they were watering.

"Leave me alone," I said. I went back to my room and slammed the door behind me. That was the slap I would've liked to give her back.

I was feeling something indescribable. Not just sadness, but bewilderment or something. It's strange, but it had never occurred to me that my mother might remarry one day. For me, marriage has to be connected to love and to wanting to have children. Did she and François love each other? Personally, I'd never believed the story of their romance. I thought it was more like an arrangement between them. And the proof was, they slept in separate beds. Suddenly I wondered if they got it on together. I know it sounds lame, but I'd never asked myself the question. Because of the word "marriage," awful images suddenly started flashing through my mind: my mother naked on a bed, François working away on top of her, their two bodies, little moans and breathing mixed together like in the movies. It was gross. And I thought of my father, who was all alone. On that night, on that cursed night when it all started, I couldn't help but think about my father as I considered the implications of the word "marriage." Yes, all alone out there. What would he think of it? Wouldn't he think that we'd made a nice new life for ourselves without him, nice and cozy in a big apartment in the 16th arrondissement? If I were in his shoes, all that would make me want to puke. In any case I couldn't endorse it. It would be betraying my father. Suddenly I realized that my mother was going to take Francois's particule. She would change her name to Catherine de Courtois. Damn, that was ugly. Would I have to change my name, too? To Julien de Courtois? Never. A novelist can't just change names. It would confuse his readers. I'm Julien Parme, period. Like my father.

Ever since we'd been living in that apartment, I felt like my mother couldn't stand me anymore. And now I was learning that she wanted to marry that worthless piece of shit. I really couldn't understand why. And above all I felt it was bad for me. They wouldn't waste any time trying to get rid of me, since I didn't get along with François at all. We were always fighting, and by marrying him, my mother would inevitably take his side. It would be no different than if she'd abandoned me by the side of the road.

I stood up and went into their bedroom. I was looking for a clue. Now I saw the room differently. The funny thing is, it was actually at a wedding that the two of them met. And this is where that had led us. To shit. With Bénédicte as a bonus.

There was a photo of François on the piano. I examined it carefully. He looked like a retard with that little scarf around his neck, even when it wasn't cold. For me, that proved that my mother couldn't love the guy. Next to my father, there was no comparison. You just had to look at the pictures, and it was obvious. The only thing François had going for him was his money. As it happens, my mother always liked money, beautiful apartments, and all that stuff. It reminded me of something Marco once told me about women. According to him there was just one thing that interested them, and that was money. The proof, he said, was that all the ugly guys who have dough go out with hotties. That was why Marco wanted to go to business school after taking the baccalaureat exam.

I rummaged through their things a bit, but didn't find anything very interesting. I sat down at the piano. I tried to play a little tune of my own, but I stopped pretty soon. I'm hopeless when it comes to music. So I went to sit where my mother does her makeup. I didn't know what I was doing or exactly what I was after, but I started putting lipstick on, the way circus performers do. I was just fooling around. There was a photo of my mother stuck into the mirror's frame. She was beautiful in it. I compared my reflection in the mirror to the picture, to see if she and I really looked like each other, now that I had girl's lips. I pulled my hair back, the way she did. I don't know why, but looking at that photograph for so long made me sad. In it, my mother looked the way I saw her when I was little. I totally trusted her in those days. Things sure had changed.

I went into their bathroom and threw the whole tube of lipstick into the toilet for no special reason. I also tore the photo into a thousand pieces. I was kind of on edge. I wanted to take revenge for something, without really knowing what. "If they get married," I told myself, "I'm out of here." I felt like an orphan. That was it, like an orphan, betrayed by my mother. Then I flushed the toilet. I don't know why I did that, but as I looked at the swirling red water in the bowl, I felt I was accomplishing something important. Yeah, things sure had changed. Now I knew who my mother really was. I knew her real face. I couldn't lie to myself about that anymore. I wasn't a child anymore.

little later that night, I heard the front door slam. They were back from their dinner party. I'd been in my room for a long time. Stretched out on my bed, trying to get my thoughts straight. What time could it be? I didn't want to attract attention by turning on the light. Midnight, maybe. I waited quite a bit longer. Eventually, I started to feel a little hungry. But I didn't want to leave my room, just in case. I waited until all the lights were out, and then I got up. I was still dressed. I felt like a burglar. I scared myself. Because the thing that really scares the hell out of me is the idea of coming face to face with a burglar. It happens, apparently. No kidding. I tiptoed to the kitchen. I opened the refrigerator as if it were a safe, but there was nothing that I felt like eating, so I just poured myself a glass of milk. After one swallow, I realized I was leaving red marks on the rim. I'd forgotten to wipe the lipstick off. What an idiot! I looked at the metallic reflection of my face in the fridge door. A sad clown. Right about now, I figured that Mathilde and the others must be having fun. They were probably drinking colored cocktails and all. And there I was with my glass of milk, looking at my shiny reflection in a refrigerator. I took a deep breath. Life is unfair. I don't know why, but it made me think of the false light from long-dead stars. Then I headed for my room, dragging my feet like a man condemned to death who was actually innocent but nobody realized it.

I didn't feel like sleeping, and if there's one thing I hate, it's going to bed when I don't feel like sleeping. I toss and turn and my thoughts start racing like panicky horses, so that afterward I feel even less like sleeping than before. Sometimes I stay awake half the night. I swear. I had the feeling that was about to happen now, so I stayed in the living room, doing nothing. Sitting on the sofa waiting for the Eiffel Tower lights to go out. A pointless spectacle. Like the stars in the sky. I thought back over everything again. This had been the worst day of my life. Then I got up. I was looking for something to do. I remembered that in the beginning, during the first weeks when my mother and I came to live in this apartment, I'd visited Bénédicte a few times while she was sleeping. She usually slept in panties and a T-shirt. She looked really beautiful like that. I would stand in the darkness, a few inches away, looking at her. It made my whole body shiver.

And once I walked into the bathroom while she was taking a shower. She screamed, even though she was the one who'd forgotten to lock the door. Seriously. I saw her completely naked. How many times had I thought back on that image, which had lasted just a fraction of a second? Thousands of times, at least. I tried to drive all those thoughts out of my head, but I couldn't. So I closed my eyes and tried to imagine Mathilde taking a shower. That was playing with fire. I've always felt it's really dangerous to dream too much. It gives you false hope. And hope is what kills you, even though most people will say that's what makes them go on living.

I left the living room. What was there for me to do at that time of night? I wanted to go to Bénédicte's room, but I noticed that my mother and François weren't asleep yet. I could see a yellow line under their bedroom door. So I tiptoed back to the end of the hallway. I could hear their voices, but not very clearly. I was dying to know what they were saying; I couldn't help it. So I went into their bathroom, the one that connects to the place where my mother hangs up all her clothes—a dressing room, it's called—and hid among her coats. From where I was, I could hear snatches of their conversation.

"You're exaggerating," said François.

"I'm exaggerating? What makes you say I'm exaggerating?"

I stayed there for a while. A spy in their closet, the real thing. Then the voices stopped and the silence freaked me out. The flashes came back to haunt me. I was terrified I would start hearing suspicious noises. To calm down, I told myself: "Of course not! What are you thinking? They're old, for chrissakes! In their forties . . . Maybe their fifties, for The Particule. At that age you think about lots of things, but you don't think about that anymore. You think about your work. You read the newspaper. You listen to classical music. But not that." I wanted to leave my hiding place and go back to my room, but the closet door suddenly opened. I barely had time to bury myself in one of the fur coats hanging there. It was my mother—she was ten feet from me. Talk about stress! She was searching for something, and she angrily yanked open a couple of drawers. My heart was pounding in my chest. I was afraid you could hear it, that's how hard it was beating. If she found me there, I may as well tell you, I'd be dead. Then François walked up behind her, to the dressing room door.

"Maybe there's something we can do," he said.

"Oh yeah? Do what? I've been looking for something for years!"

"Why are you getting angry?"

"Because I can't take it anymore, you understand?"

"See, there you go again."

"No, I'm not. I'm telling you how I feel. Don't you see what kind of an atmosphere we're living in? I don't know; I've run out of patience."

"You say that because you're afraid of how he'll react."

"I'm not asking his opinion about it. I'm not afraid of anything. It's my decision, isn't it? No, that's not it. I tell you, the problem is that I've run out of patience."

My mother walked past him without turning around. At that, François closed the door and followed her. I could still hear their voices. They were continuing their discussion on the other side. I was shaking, without quite knowing why. I got the impression they were talking about me. Why had she run out of patience? Because I'd gotten bad grades? Or been busted for smoking? Either that, or she'd noticed that her photo had disappeared. Yeah, that must be it. Shit. I suddenly imagined that the goddamn toilet hadn't completely swallowed what I'd thrown in it, despite my flushing it and all. Maybe that was how she'd figured out that I'd torn up her photo. Why the heck had I done that, anyway? I felt conflicted: I was so freaked out about being caught that I wanted to go back to my room, but at the same time my curiosity was too strong.

I must admit that I even considered stepping out of my hiding place and admitting that I knew everything about the marriage business. Telling them they didn't have to worry about my reaction, because Bénédicte had already let the cat out of the bag. I was even this close to telling them that I thought it was a good idea, because I loved her. Yeah, I actually wanted to tell my mother that. Kind of shows you how cracked I was. But I'm sure it was because of what I had just heard. I had become a kid again, and I wanted to run crying to my mother's arms to be forgiven. But as I approached the door, she continued: "I don't know what's happened. He wasn't that way before. He was more . . . I don't know. When I look at him I can't help but think of his father, you see. In fact, the older he gets, the more he looks like him. It's a horrible thing to say, but that's the way it is. He's got the same unnerving look. He lies all the time, for example. He lies constantly. And he steals money. Do you realize that? He steals in his own house."

"He's young," François tried to point out.

"It has nothing to do with his age. It's deeper than that. I've run out of patience, I tell you. I can't stand him anymore. He exhausts me. You know perfectly well that he does it to drive me crazy. Don't you understand? It's because he's angry at me. Because of his father, and everything that happened back then. And after we're married, it will just get worse."

"That's why I'm telling you that we may have to do something."

"Like what?"

"Why don't you send him to stay with his uncle in Nice? Didn't he suggest that to you?"

"That's not possible. He travels all year long. Anyway, it's too complicated."

"Well, there's always the possibility of that school we talked about."

"I know . . ."

I stepped away from the door. I swallowed painfully. I left the dressing room by way of the bathroom. I didn't know what to do anymore. I just stood motionless for a while. No idea. Totally bummed. I felt as if something inside me was tearing, as if someone had given me a huge punch in the stomach. That's the effect it had on me. I was having trouble catching my breath. Then I went back to my room, locked the door, and sat down on my bed. I tried to breathe calmly, but I couldn't. My hands were even shaking a little. Not much, just a little. I thought back on what I'd just heard. What a bitch! I told myself. She couldn't stand me anymore, that's what she'd said. She thought I looked more and more like my father, and she hated both of us. That was it: she hated us. I hated her, too. Everybody in this dump hated each other.

I'd never have imagined she could talk about me that way. I knew I drove her up the wall. I'd heard her say on the phone that I was having a so-called difficult adolescence, and that it was no picnic. But I'd never have thought she'd say such shitty things about me, I swear. Had I missed something? I was trying to understand what they meant. Like, what was this thing that I had to do? The school . . . Suddenly I thought about Ben, a guy I used to hang out with at school. He'd also had problems with his parents because he didn't do anything in class and kept screwing up. So his parents sent him to a military boarding school a long way from Paris, like in the Alps. A hard-ass place. Wake-up at six a.m. and all. With guys who were barely literate. The counselors would slap you around if you didn't toe the line, and they even crawled into your bunk after dark, supposedly. Ben came back to Paris for vacation once, looking as depressed as shit. We got together one afternoon and he told me. It would have blown your mind. It was called Les Roches Noires, and Ben said it was worse than hell. A kind of prison, but not a prison like the Institut, a real one. Without Madame Thomas. And just for kids. Damn. Maybe that's what the two of them were thinking about: getting rid of me. I knew perfectly well that my mother thought I created a lousy mood at home. She'd criticized me for it tons of times. If she sent me to boarding school at Roches Noires, I'd certainly be less of a problem for her. I suddenly felt panicky, let me tell you. I felt like people were setting traps for me at night, when I was supposed to be sleeping. I felt betrayed. Anyway, I'd known for a long time that there wasn't anybody in this place who wished me well. At best, they would've liked to see me dead.

I stood up. Still shaking, I got undressed. Well, I changed my shirt. I didn't know what I wanted to do yet but, it was like a reflex: I had to run away. From the closet I took my black jacket, the one I love. I looked around like a thousand times so as not to forget something important. I put a notebook and a pencil in my pocket. Then I went into the bathroom—my bathroom, this time. I decided not to turn on the light, so as not to be spotted. I put on some deodorant. And a little cologne, some green tea stuff I'd ordered for Christmas. It was weird to be making those everyday gestures as I began to understand what I was about to do.

Then I went to the foyer, where the coats are hung up. I searched pretty thoroughly. In François's raincoat, I found his wallet. He ought to put his stuff away. I inspected it quickly. Damn. No bills. So I took his credit card. Too bad for him. The card was perfect. I knew the code; he'd keyed it in several times in front of me, and I'd memorized it. I was shaking. But I wasn't afraid. It was just my hands, they were shaking all by themselves. Like crazy. I couldn't help it. I thought back to my mother. She'd called me a thief when here I'd just learned that she was going to marry the guy only for his money. It made me almost crazy. Because it isn't necessarily worse to bullshit someone a little than to tell some guy, "I love you" just for his money. Guilty people are always the ones to point the finger at you. And screw it all, anyway! If they got married, that dough would become my family's, right? Wouldn't Bénédicte become my stepsister? Because in that case, it was also my step-money. There was no reason to sweat it. No reason to be shaking. After all, I was an adult now. I wasn't about to let them send me to Roches Noires without a fight. I put the card in my inside jacket pocket. From then on, I didn't have any more doubts. I opened the door as quietly as possible and closed it behind me just as quietly, using my fingertips. My heart was pounding like a guy trapped under the ice of a frozen lake. It was going boom! boom! boom! loud enough to wake the whole neighborhood. Out on the landing, I wanted to take the elevator, for once, but I was afraid it would make even more of a racket. So I hauled ass down the stairs. To get outside as fast as possible. Into the mysterious night. Out of range. Out of reach.

Part II

The Departure

Chapter 8

It was the first time I'd done something like this, taking off in the middle of the night. The novelty of the situation briefly excited me, but once I reached the building entryway, I had a moment of doubt. What was I going to do? The fact was, I didn't even know where Emilie Fermat's birthday party was, except that she lived somewhere near the Champs-Élysées. Maybe I could phone Marco. Or at worst just wander around until dawn. But what would happen if I got caught? The parents would kill me, tomorrow morning, no doubt about it. And after that, they'd have every reason in the world to ship me off somewhere, like to Les Roches Noires. I had to face facts. If I left now I wouldn't be able to come home again, ever. This wasn't a casual thing, some little two-bit escapade. No, it was a lot more than that. I stood in the entryway for a while, thinking. Maybe it would be better to go back up to my room. After all, I had come this far. Making it to the front door of the building was something. I'd proven to myself that I could leave in the middle of the night if I felt like it. "All right," I thought. "Maybe I shouldn't screw around too much now." Besides, I was starting to feel tired. But then I remembered all the things I'd heard my mother saying about me. They were like a knife in my heart, and enough to make me push the building door open. I wasn't just feeling sadness, but also a sort of really strong anger. I didn't have any choice. I had to leave, and for as long as possible. Not just take a little stroll around the block. Really leave.

The street was deserted. It must've been about one in the morning. I felt like having a cigarette, to give myself courage. But at the same time, I was really afraid of running into someone from the neighborhood. Like some guy who would recognize me and call the cops. Damn. That idea stressed me out some more. My heart started pounding again. I had to calm down, or I was going to drop dead of a heart attack in the middle of the night. The best thing would be to get away from there as fast as possible. On the Champs, I would be in no danger, since my parents weren't the kind of people to know people who go out on the Champs in the middle of the night. In the middle of the night, the people my parents know are mostly asleep. Dullsville.

I headed for the métro, practically running. There was no one in the street (besides me). I was in a hurry to get the hell away from there. I don't know why, it just seemed smarter. The streets all around our apartment were still part of my mother's spider web. Especially since they may have already realized I wasn't in my room anymore. I could imagine her taking a last look around the apartment, the way she sometimes did before she went to bed. Or else getting up when she heard a suspicious noise in the hallway, like when I closed the door behind me. Seeing my bed empty would blow her mind. She would understand what had happened. But she'd immediately call the cops. That's the way my mother is, right away going for the wrong solution. And in that case it wouldn't take them long to find me if I stayed in the neighborhood, I can tell you. I'd be dragged back home. Or else they would take me to the station to cool my heels until dawn. That's the law, and the destiny of delinquency. Either way, as soon as Monday rolled around I would be deported to Les Roches Noires. In other words, to hell.

What could I do to avoid all that? At the moment, I really couldn't deal with the question. I didn't have a plan. The only thing I wanted was to run away. And my idea was to catch up with Marco at Emilie Fermat's birthday party, of course. That gave me a goal, something concrete. And it allowed me to really consider what sort of mess I was getting myself into. One thing at a time, I told myself. First, find them; after that, we'd see. I was overcome by a sudden feeling of freedom. I realized I could do anything I wanted. Absolutely anything. I had money, thanks to the credit card. I was free. That thought cheered me up, even if I wasn't really happy deep down, since I was sad. But still . . . If I felt like smoking, for example, I could withdraw cash from the ATM and buy myself cigarettes. Ten tons of cartons, if I felt like it. I thought of Marco's face, seeing me show up at the party. It cracked me up in advance. He would understand that he had made a slight mistake. See, that was typical of old Marco.

You tell him that maybe you're not going to come to the party, and right away he figures your mother has grounded you, as if you were still a baby. He always likes to think that other people are babies, as a way of building himself up. That's typical of him. And thanks to the credit card, I could even bring a bottle. Very classy. Champagne, if I wanted to. A whole bottle, I didn't care: I could certainly afford it. My laugh echoed along avenue Mozart, and it scared me, because of the resonance and the echoes, so I started walking even faster, turning right into rue La Fontaine.

The streets didn't look anything like the way they did in the daytime. I looked at the darkened buildings all around me, sheltering lives of slippers and sleeping pills. A crappy neighborhood, if you ask me. At this hour, the lights in the windows were all out, and it gave me a strange feeling. As if everyone was living in a gigantic dormitory. I imagined all those people lying next to each other, waiting to croak some day. Most of them had no trouble falling asleep. They weren't insomniacs or worrywarts. They didn't ask themselves too many questions, just the ones that don't keep you up at night. The other ones, like why we exist, they preferred not to ask. For them, when it was time to sleep, they slept. No problem. In any case, they didn't give a damn that life was rotten and that things were turning sinistrous. They'd rather get a good night's sleep. Not like me. I felt even more that I was in the right place. I didn't feel like sleeping.

Think of a dog you've tied to a post with a leash. One day, after the dog's been tugging on it, suppose the leash snaps. Naturally, the dog won't feel like sleeping. On the contrary, he'll dash off into the night like a madman.

I spotted a cash machine in the distance. It was glowing. You would have thought it was a lighthouse in the darkness. So that boats didn't wreck their hulls, to be found dashed upon the rocks the next morning—like hopes often are. At the ATM, there was already a guy keying in his code. He was practically stretched across the machine to keep anyone from seeing. A paranoid. I stood a few yards away, so as not to bother him, but he turned toward me anyway, probably to see what I looked like. You can spot robbers right off the bat, just by looking at them. Me, for example, you can tell right away that I'm not a robber. Just the same, he said, "You got a problem?" "No," I shot back. And I looked away and waited for him to finish. The stress of my life. He stuffed his bills into his coat and walked off, hugging the walls. A suspicious character, if you ask me.

In turn, I stuck in my card—well, François's. I didn't feel too confident. For all I knew, there are cameras and everything around cash machines. I punched in the code as fast as I could. How much should I withdraw? Maybe it was best not to take too much at once. It's never safe to wander around at night carrying your whole bankroll. Because holding up one guy is a lot easier than robbing an entire bank. I settled on forty euros, for starters. I looked right, left, right, right again, then left and right, and left—to make sure no one was walking toward me. Luckily, the street was empty. I removed the card, and the bills came out. Piece of cake. I gulped, then headed up the street toward the boulevard Pérphérique, because that's where the nearest métro station is. Well, nearest in a manner of speaking, because everything in this arrondissement is far from everything else, so nothing is close, except the police station.

As I was walking, it occurred to me that it might be smarter to phone Marco right away instead of waiting until I got to Emilie Fermat's neighborhood to find out where the birthday party was. But I didn't have a cell or a phone card. So I walked to the end of rue La Fontaine, because I knew that the bistro there was one of the last places on Earth that still had a pay telephone. I'd lost my cell phone. My mother originally gave it to me as a gift. She was pretending to be nice, but I knew very well she figured it would be a way for her to call me whenever she felt like it. With the cell, it was like wearing an electronic ankle bracelet. But I just called people all the time, and the monthly bill went through the roof. It drove my mother nuts. But it wasn't just me; all the kids my age did the same thing. But then it got stolen, or I lost it. Either way, I hadn't been able to call anyone for the last two weeks. It felt like being a deaf mute.

Walking along, I realized something I'd never realized before: that the La Fontaine of the rue La Fontaine was actually the La Fontaine of La Fontaine's *Fables*. You know, the guy who wrote "The Grasshopper and the Crow," for example. Some things really hit you, at night. So I started daydreaming: maybe there would be a rue Julien-Parme some day. Or an avenue, rather, because I like trees. People would walk along it, feeling sad. The author has been dead for a century, but we still miss him. Because I forgot to mention that I'm writing for posterity. That's right. Maybe there would be a plaque on François's building, made out of marble and all, with "Julien Parme lived here" written on it. Some girls would be in front of it, weeping. Nobody would mention The Particule, on the other hand. If you wanted to see a plaque about him, you'd have to go to the cemetery.

Chapter 9

I went into the bistro. There was hardly anybody inside, of course. Just two guys drinking at the counter. Most of the chairs were turned upside down on the tables. The mood really sort of hit you. The waiter gave me a nasty look. I asked him if he was still selling cigarettes. He pointed to a package of Marlboro Lights and said, "That's all we've got." I usually hate Lights, because everybody smokes them, I swear. But I wasn't about to be fussy at one in the morning. So I pulled out a twenty-euro bill, just like that. I even impressed myself. The waiter gave me another dirty look. He must not like having to make change. So I added, "Could I have a beer, too?" Again, he said nothing. I went to sit at a table. After all, I had plenty of time. No need to switch neighborhoods right away, since I had the whole night ahead of me.

Suddenly I had a terrific idea: to write a novel I would call *The Whole Night Ahead of Me*. It would tell the story of a guy who's running away. A super original thing. An Italian journalist knocks on my office door. She wants to interview me. Usually, I turn everybody down. But this journalist is a real beauty, so I open the door, with a glass of whiskey in my hand. I'm very depressed. Very, very depressed—circles under my eyes, and all. She follows me into my lair, moved by the thought that this is where I compose my prose. She settles into an armchair facing me and starts right off with a classic question: "Monsieur Parme, this fabulous novel, which is considered at the international scale and in the entire world as the greatest novel of the 21st century— of course I mean *The Whole Night Ahead of Me*—can one say that it's autobiographical?" At that, I sigh deeply before answering. What's the point of this whole charade? I wonder. After a while, you wind up knowing journalists' questions by heart. And you know that the essence lies elsewhere. Even if you have to play the media game. "In the etymological sense of the word, yes, you can. In the Greek sense, of course . . ." After the interview, I ask her what she has planned next. Her answer is pretty clever: "Nothing. I have the whole night ahead of me." I give her a sad smile and she smiles back at me, because she understands that I want to find a little consolation in her arms. To escape the urge to kill myself for a few hours. Afterward, she writes her damned article sitting naked in the kitchen. It makes the front page of the newspaper in Italy next to a picture of me looking suicidal, with my desperate gaze and my fingers yellowed by cigarettes.

As it happens, I had just lit myself one. I was daydreaming and all. I'd really like to be depressed . . . Just then, the two guys sitting at the counter turned around, as if they could read my mind, and started laughing. Was it something about me? It was probably because of my age. They must've been wondering what the hell I was doing here, practically in the middle of the night. Then one of them whispered something into the waiter's ear. Right away he turned toward me as if to check, and then he started laughing too. They were plotting something. Damn. I started freaking out. Maybe they were saying that I had money on me, and all. I wouldn't have a chance against three of them. Finally the waiter came and set my beer down with the change. He was still looking at me mockingly, the big jerk. I bet he'd never read a single one of La Fontaine's fables, and here he was acting like a wise guy in front of me. As a distraction, I politely asked him if they had a pay phone. He gestured with his chin to a door at the other end of the counter, near the restrooms. Really not very talkative, the guy. All right. I didn't touch my beer, because I didn't much like the look of those guys. I got up to go call Marco. I put a euro in the slot and dialed the number. Because it was a pay phone, it made me feel like being in an old black-and-white movie.

I was afraid I'd get his voicemail, but luckily it rang. But it was ringing in empty space, and I wound up getting his voicemail anyway. Shit. I hung up. He probably couldn't hear his phone ringing over the music. I tried again. He still didn't pick up, so I left a message: "Hey, Marco, it's Julien. What the hell are you up to? I've been trying to reach you for hours! Listen, I may come join you . . . I wanted to find out if the party was fun . . . And also, where it was. Because I forgot the place . . . Emilie

Fermat's address, I mean . . . So try to pick up if you hear your ringtone. I'll call you back in half an hour, okay? The time it takes for me to get to the Champs. All right, so long."

Then I called Information to ask for the Fermats' address, but the woman couldn't find anything under that name. Unlisted number, she said. Since appearing in her movie, Emilie Fermat apparently thought she was Sharon Stone. She must've asked her parents to get an unlisted number. Nothing pisses me off more than that. If you have a phone, it's so people can call you, right? In any case, Emilie Fermat was the kind of person who thinks her shit doesn't stink. The truth is, if she were only half as beautiful as she thought she was, I think she'd still be doing very well. She thought she was really well known, but if she were well known, people would know it—by definition.

I was a little worried when I went back to the main room, and the guys at the bar started laughing again. To make it clear that I was indifferent to their sarcasm, I drank my beer down all at once. What with the wine I'd drunk a little earlier, my head was really starting to spin. But not too much. Because I can hold my liquor. As a writer, I mean. Then I had another idea. I would call someone from my German class who might have the student list, and therefore Mathilde's address. A good plan. And that's how I thought of Hervé Morvin.

I better tell you right away that Hervé Morvin was a real dork. I wouldn't want to be in his parents' shoes. Or in his, either, considering the way he looked. He was always snitching on people and sucking up to the teachers by doing exercises that weren't assigned, or talking about books he had supposedly read in the original German. In other words, a total hypocrite. Here's proof: instead of using a book bag for his school things like everybody else, he carried a leather briefcase with folders inside. The sort of thing a banker or even a cabinet minister would carry. You got the impression that the guy was running half the country. He really took himself seriously. I'd have never thought I'd be telephoning his place. Just shows how surprising life is. I went back to the restrooms. I asked Information for the number of Monsieur and Madame Morvin, in Paris. They offered to connect me, and a moment later the phone was ringing in my pal Hervé's apartment. I was super excited, convinced that I'd had the idea of the century. Which tells you that I don't hold my liquor all that well. Anyway, a woman answered. In a voice like Jacques Chirac's, I asked if she was Madame Morvin.

"Who is calling?"

"The President of the Republic," I almost answered, dying with laughter. But when I heard her voice I suddenly realized that it was really late and that Morvin had probably gone to bed ages ago. I don't really know why, but I thought I was going to be tracked down, like a guy on the run. It made me feel so panicky, I hung up without answering her. Then I stood in front of the phone for a while, thinking about calling back. As a pretext, I could say that we'd been cut off, bad connection and all, then move straight on to Morvin, really insisting that she wake him up, something like, "It's a matter of life and death, madame."

That would have been wild. But I wasn't too sure that old lady Morvin had a sense of humor. And I probably wouldn't get through to Hervé anyway. Calling so late hadn't been such a good idea after all.

I paid a visit to the bathroom and splashed some water on my face. A small mirror was hanging on the wall. That's when I got it: I was still wearing the damn lipstick, which was smeared across my chin. That's probably why the two idiots at the bar were laughing at me. I wiped it off with some water from the faucet. Good thing I'd seen that before running into Mathilde Fermat. Because that would've been the humiliation of my life, I can tell you. But would I even get to see her? I hoped Marco would answer his damn phone the next time I called.

I went back to the main room. The two guys looked me over. When I walked by them, the short one with the bad haircut said something I wasn't quite sure I got: "So you went to clean yourself up, honeybunch?" Very funny. No, really. Very funny. I chose not to answer. I am indifferent to sarcasm. Like La Fontaine. The two of us, we never answer crude people. That's the way it is. A matter of principle, for a writer.

"Hey there! I'm talking to you."

I pretended not to hear. No kidding. I went to sit down and lit myself a second cigarette. To make it clear I paid them no more attention than the ant paid the fox in the fable (though without being a show-off with my quotations).

Then I got up.

"Hey, you leaving already?"

This was no time to get into a discussion to explain that the lipstick was a misunderstanding. Instead, I decided to leave the bistro really casually. Like a gentleman, even. I'm not someone who goes looking for fights, if you want to know. I'm anti-violence. Especially when it's just me against three guys. I walked for ten yards and once I was far enough away, I turned around and gave them the finger. Then I started running like crazy without daring to look back. I stopped at the end of the street, completely out of breath. Those guys got what they had coming. A pair of perverts, for sure.

I walked for at least ten more minutes without seeing a single person. Totally deserted. It was really weird to see the neighborhood so empty. It looked completely different at night. Then I got to the métro station, but it was closed. That's when I remembered that the métro doesn't run all night long. Conductors have to sleep too, after all, to be in shape for the days when they go on strike. So there was only one thing left to do: take a taxi. As a general rule I wasn't really in the habit of taking taxis, but this was different. I still had thirty euros, at least. I told myself that there couldn't be a whole lot of fourteen-, almost fifteen-year-old guys with thirty euros in their pockets wandering around at that time of night. The idea really appealed to me. To be the only one out walking at night. Yeah. Still, I didn't feel like walking forever. So I went and stood at the taxi stand, which was deserted, too. No problem. I could wait. And I lit myself another cigarette, frowning.

I waited, but didn't see any taxis. If this went on much longer, I'd make it in time for Emilie Fermat's thirtieth. I started to get impatient. So I decided to walk there. After all, the Champs weren't that far. You just had to walk. And so that's how I happened to be walking toward the Champs.

At one point, on a big avenue whose name I've forgotten, I spotted a woman waiting on the sidewalk. Right away, I told myself maybe she was a professional—of the ass, if you know what I mean. And at that thought, I felt like a fire was flaring up in my belly, and big flames rising up my throat. It scared me to walk by her like that, so I thought I'd cross to the other side. But then I saw another woman across the street. Damn! I was cornered. I tried to stay calm, but I couldn't, because now I had one on my right and one on my left, and all sorts of strange ideas were running through my mind. So I continued looking straight ahead, like real cool, while doing weird contortions with my eyes, like a chameleon, so I could check them out just the same. Because they fascinated me a little. Especially since I had money on me, for once.

It reminded me of that time the year before, when I wandered like a lost sole through Pigalle. I was obsessed by the stuff you saw there. Here's what I did: I walked up the boulevard, back down, then back up again, pretending to be in a big hurry and not even noticing that the sidewalks were crawling with peep shows. I did this thousands of times, but was too shy to stop. I had developed a hypersharp technique that allowed me to scope out everything around while seeming to be looking straight ahead. It was actually the same technique I used during quizzes to scope out my classmates' answers. The chameleon technique.

When I walked by the woman, she didn't say anything to me at all. Just like that. It took my breath away. As if she had suggested I come and make love with her. The stress of my life. After that, I picked up my pace toward the Champs. (Marco once told me that he had tried it, with a hooker. I swear. So as not to take any chances, he'd put on two condoms, one on top of the other. That detail cracked me up. One on top of the other. Because condoms apparently break unexpectedly. With Marco's technique, you're sure not to catch anything dirty. Clever, isn't it? One on top of the other. Like when you put on two sweaters on a really cold day.) After a few dozen yards, I turned around. The woman was still waiting at the same spot. And I told myself that when you paid for a woman, maybe that's also what you're paying for, the idea that someone had been waiting for you in the cold, in spite of the darkness and the danger—the idea, even if it was ridiculous or untrue—that someone was waiting for you.

I walked for at least twenty minutes before I saw the Champs-Élysées, all lit up. It almost felt like early evening. Or even mid-afternoon. The world upside down, in other words. It made me happy to see that. I felt less alone. People were strolling on the sidewalks, and some of the restaurants were still open.

The opposite of the 16th arrondissement, in other words. I walked to the first open pizzeria I saw. I figured a pizzeria would probably have a pay phone. You're probably wondering why. The answer is simple: pizza is mainly for poor people, and so are pay phones. Elementary. Anyway, that's what I told myself, surrounded by the sleepless flood of people who weren't asleep yet, in spite of the late hour, but who would lately soon be sleeping, I imagine, since it was already super late—and allow me to dedicate that sentence to the Académie française.

I've got an inside track.

The Champs isn't anything like what people think. I don't want to show off my culture by using too many quotations, but somebody, a Polish writer of the last century I think, said it was the most beautiful avenue in the world. I don't agree with him at all, but in my opinion the guy who said that, the Pole, also agreed with me, even if he wrote the opposite. It's just that he figured that if everybody said that, we'd be cleared of the Japanese and the yokels. Because if you tell the Japanese and the yokels that it's the most beautiful avenue in the world, they'll naturally head there right away. It's like a reflex. This way, we get to stroll peacefully around much prettier parts of Paris without being bothered by them. Saint-Sulpice, for example. That's what I think.

Was Mathilde really going with that creep Marco?

In the pizzeria, I asked one of the waiters if they had a pay phone, but the guy walked by me without answering. Typical Italian behavior. And yet I want to say right out that I love pizza, even if that doesn't have anything to do with anything. Anyway, I stood there waiting like a jerk in the middle of the restaurant for a few minutes, thinking he was going to come back to answer me after delivering his plates and stuff. But I got fed up with waiting, so I went to the restrooms to see. Restrooms were sort of my specialty that night. I searched everywhere, but no telephone. Shit. On the other hand, I did see something funny: a guy who had apparently lost a coin to a condom vending machine. He was furiously pounding on the dispenser, which now had him by the balls. I figured he didn't have any more change, and his girlfriend was probably waiting for him back at their table, and had no idea what he was plotting. If I had a dinner date with a girl, I'd never take her to a lousy joint like this. I was tempted to offer the guy a euro in exchange for letting me use his cell phone. Everybody has a cell today except me, since mine was stolen. But I was too shy to say anything. So I went back to the main room.

I didn't know quite what to do next. And that's when the most unbelievable thing of the evening happened: at a table in the back I spotted my French teacher, Madame Thomas. I swear, I'm not making this up—Madame Thomas, in person. I hesitated for a moment. It might actually have been smart to hide, seeing as how I was running away from home. But I just stood there, gazing at her the way you'd look at a landscape.

She was all alone. Oh boy, I thought to myself. It had never really occurred to me that she also had a life outside of the school. Looking back now, I think that by standing there without moving like that, I was waiting for her to look my way, and see me first. I didn't know what else to do, in any case. I didn't have any place to go. That's when I remembered the first time I had seen Madame Thomas. It had been three weeks after school started. Originally, Monsieur Vigouse was supposed to teach the class, like I already told you. But he had an accident. We never knew exactly what. There we were, jumping for joy, and for all we knew a métro had run over him. (In any case, the only time teachers make other people happy is when they get sick and classes are canceled.) Rumor had it that he'd been hit by a car while peacefully walking along the sidewalk. Death can come at any moment. We should never forget that. But we often live as if we have time ahead of us. We walk along the sidewalks, whistling.

Anyway. After Monsieur Vigouse, we didn't have French class for a week. And then on the next Monday, Madame Thomas appeared. She fascinated me right away. She walked to the dais, really calm and all, wearing a skirt and that sheer blouse of hers. She put down her things and said, "All right. Starting today, I'll be teaching this class." Her approach shook me up.

After I'd been standing motionless in the middle of the pizza place for a while, Madame Thomas finally turned, and our eyes met. She gave me a big smile, a really nice smile, but I could tell she was uncomfortable, and probably wondering what the hell I was doing there. It's true that the situation was improbable. I walked over to her shyly.

"Good evening, Julien," she said. "What are you doing here?"

"I'm going to a party," I answered, feeling pretty proud of myself.

I was in luck: for once that I was going to a party, she was there to witness it. To impress her some more, I added, "On the Champs." But right away I realized that maybe I should have lied. Because of my running away.

"But don't you have class tomorrow?" she said, looking at her watch. She must have forgotten it was a teacher training day, which is what I told her. So as not to talk about school too much, I quickly followed up with:

"Did you have dinner here?"

She gave a small, odd smile.

"Yes."

"Oh? Do you like pizza?"

"No, not that much."

What else could I say to her? I tried to think of a topic of conversation. A literary example or the title of a novel. Something to make a good impression—and a distraction. But I couldn't come up with anything. In the meantime, I said, "Pizza isn't really to my taste, either." Then I lit a cigarette and offered her one. She seemed to hesitate. She probably felt awkward at accepting a cigarette from one of her students. I almost told her I was quitting school, to put her at ease about the cigarette. But I didn't need to, because she finally took it. That really rattled me. I lit her cigarette right away.

"Did you eat here too?"

I imagined myself telling her that actually I had just in come to find a telephone, to make a call (logical), because my cell phone had been stolen in a fairly violent fight in which I had done pretty well, considering the number of guys who jumped me, even if I hadn't been able to keep from losing my cell and getting a bloody eyebrow (nothing serious, luckily). I hadn't been able to find a phone in this restaurant, but anyway if she felt like it she could come with me to that girl Emilie Fermat's birthday party. Man, I would really have liked to see the look on Marco's face! But in the end, I opted for a more synthetic answer:

"Er, no. Actually I was looking for a phone. I absolutely have to reach some friends, and I hoped there might be one in this restaurant."

She suggested that I use her cell. Just like that. Which proves that she was really a nice teacher, who thought of helping her students when she could. I was touched, and I accepted. But at the same time, I didn't feel at all like leaving anymore. I would've liked to spend hours like this, across from her, looking at her. Discussing literature. Or weeping in her arms while I told her about everything that had been happening to me. I dialed Marco's number. Suddenly I heard his voice. Hallelujah! But my heart wasn't in it anymore.

"Hello?"

". . ."

"Hello?"

"..."

He wasn't able to hear anything over the music.

"Can you hear me?"

"Yeah, I can hear you now. Who is it?"

"It's me."

"Who?"

"It's Julien!"

I felt embarrassed. I really didn't want Madame Thomas to hear. But at the same time I had to scream because of the music. In fact I was yelling so loud, the whole restaurant could follow what I was saying.

"Listen, I have to go to another party, with some famous friends, but I wanted to come by and say hello before going somewhere else."

"Where the hell are you?" yelled Marco.

"What? On the Champs."

"I see. And you're coming over?"

"Yeah . . . Just to say hello. After that, I've got another thing. A party with my writer friends."

I glanced over at Madame Thomas to savor the impression I was making.

"What? All right. So you're coming! Are you alone or are you with your Charlotte?"

"A sort of seminar around Kafkaf."

Another discreet glance.

"What?"

"Exactly. For the review I write regularly for."

"What are you talking about?"

"No, no. Under a pseudonym."

"I don't understand a word you're saying, Jules."

"Uh-huh . . . Uh-huh . . ."

"All right, listen, it's rue Pierre-Charron. Know it?"

"Uh-huh . . . Uh-huh . . ."

"Can you hear me? Number 13. You don't need a code. Just press the buzzer for Fermat. Got that?"

"Uh-huh . . . Uh-huh . . . Very interesting."

"Okay? Good. It's cool that you're able to come. We'll have fun, you'll see! It's a hell of a party. Lots of girls!"

"Very well. I'll talk to my publisher about it."

"What?"

"You're very welcome. See you later."

I hung up, delighted with my trick. Madame Thomas was looking at me oddly. I thanked her for letting me use her phone. It was really nice of her. I would've liked to check my messages too, but that would've felt like asking too much. Besides, I wasn't quite myself anymore. My heart was pounding. After all, here I was with Madame Thomas in a Champs Élysées restaurant at one in the morning—with no ulterior motives, it should be said. I couldn't get over it. For all I knew, we would wind up out on the sidewalk together. Everything would look beautiful to me, even the pathetic bare trees growing out of the concrete. I'd offer to take her home in a taxi, to drop her off at her place, and she'd draw close as we were about to say good-bye, and then come closer still, still closer, and instead of giving me a peck on the cheek, our lips would touch and then we'd kiss with our tongues and all, and she'd ask me up to her apartment—meaning up to her bedroom—and we'd find ourselves in an elevator that was too narrow for my love, and we'd kiss again and again, until the moment came when we'd slip under her covers and I would recite a few verses for her.

What does a woman her age think about? I mean a woman who is thirty, at least. I mean, does she dream at night of sleeping with a guy who's fourteen, almost fifteen? Because I've spent thousands of hours in the imaginary arms of women her age. I know it happens, sometimes. In my opinion, female pedophilia should be encouraged. Especially since Madame Thomas had beautiful eyes. I should make a move, I told myself. In my dreams. I could ask her to go have a drink somewhere. At her place, say. If she hesitated, I could tell her the truth. That this might be the last time we would see each other, since I wasn't planning to come back to the Institut, and that I was running away. But of course I was too chicken for that. In Pigalle, I hadn't even dared stop in front of a peep show, so suggesting something like that to a real woman was unthinkable. Actually, I *was* thinking of it, but I knew I'd never have the guts to do it.

To keep the conversation going, and also to justify my standing in front of her without doing anything, I asked her if she was happy at the Institut. It was either that or the weather, and I don't know shit about the weather.

"Pretty much. What about you?"

"Me?"

JULIEN PARME · 101

"Yes. Are you happy there?"

I was afraid of screwing up. I decided to play it safe.

"Not really. I find most of the classes boring. Except for French, which is my favorite subject."

She smiled. I felt she was teasing me a little, as if I was saying that to suck up to her. But all you had to do was to look at my report card: aside from French, I didn't do a damned thing. So I decided to be more specific:

"It's the only subject that has a connection with real life, I think. That's what I like about literature."

"Do you read?"

"Constantly," I answered, puffing as if it exhausted me physically.

"Oh? What kind of books?"

"Actually, desperate books that move me, especially."

"Desperate books . . . Why?"

Another faintly amused smile. I was immediately sorry I'd said that.

"I have a fairly optimistic nature and all, but when you read a book about happiness, with a phony ending where everything comes out okay, you have the feeling that you're excluded from that happiness. Whereas to the contrary, in a really desperate book, I don't know, you find someone who suffers the way you do, who has the same troubles, sort of like a brother in a way, then it doesn't hurt so much."

I had poured all that out without thinking, and felt a little apprehensive about her reaction. She looked at me strangely, because of the mishmash I'd just dished out to her, so I added: "Though I also like books that end well." And since I felt I looked stupid, I concluded, "But of course that depends," before finally shading it with the classic, "Anyway, I don't know."

Right then, the guy I had seen in the restroom—the one from the condom dispenser—walked over to our table. I was wondering what he wanted when Madame Thomas introduced us. He was her boyfriend. I swear. I was totally embarrassed. Especially since he was at least forty years old. Maybe more. I suddenly felt pitiful. He looked at me the way you'd look at a small turd on the edge of the sidewalk. I almost considered lending him a coin for the dispenser, while asking if it didn't bother him to be calmly plotting to jump the woman of my dreams. But I understood that I had to leave them. He looked surprised to see me still up at this hour, too. As if I were twelve years old. That really pissed me off. Grown-ups don't understand a damn thing most of the time. In any case he didn't think for a moment that I could be a rival, that I was a man too, and that it was really depressing to see myself as if I were a kid who ought to be in pajamas, considering the hour.

So I said good-bye to Madame Thomas, feeling a little sad and all, and putting as much gravity into it as I could. I wanted her to understand that this was farewell. Because I couldn't come back to the Institut, of course, given the situation. But she couldn't know that yet. I would miss her. She seemed troubled. As if she understood that it might have worked out, between the two of us. Then I thanked her for lending me her phone. I left the restaurant full of conflicting feelings. It was strange. I didn't know what to think anymore. Out on the sidewalk, I closed my eyes to really preserve the last image I would ever have of her. After all, she had taught me many things. I had worked on all my essays to please her, for example. But I had to face facts: I was fourteen, almost fifteen. I didn't measure up. Not yet. And then I said to myself: "Just the same, it's crazy to run into her like that in the middle of the night. Right in the middle of Paris. It's really a funny bit of luck." It's true, when you think of it: it was crazy. But I don't believe in luck. What about La Fontaine; did he believe in luck? I wondered as I went on my way. Probably not. As a writer, I mean. I think he must've especially believed in destiny. Like me. In any case, most of the time it's easy: La Fontaine and I, we agree on everything. Him, especially.

Chapter 10

After that, I walked to rue Pierre-Charron. I was feeling keyed up, mainly from meeting Madame Thomas but also because it was a new experience for me to be roaming around like that in the middle of the night. I felt everybody was looking at me and asking, "What's he doing up at this hour?" But I knew perfectly well that nobody actually was paying any attention to me. I tried not to think too hard about what I was doing. I knew that I was screwing up at the outer limits of screw-ups. What would happen tomorrow morning? It occurred to me that François might freeze his credit card when he realized I'd swiped it. The solution, which I hadn't thought of earlier, was to stock up on cash right away—make a big score. Otherwise I'd run out of money pretty fast. And then I'd have to go home or find work to get by, and since I don't have my driver's license yet, I'd wind up working as a cashier in a grocery store. So that was it: the next cash machine was mine.

I stopped in front of Pierre-Charron number 13. The door to the building was open, so I walked in and crossed the inner courtyard. Right away, I could tell where the party was, because music was blasting from the sixth-floor windows. It was so loud, it hurt your ears. You almost wanted to ask for a minute of silence, just for the neighbors. But maybe Emilie Fermat had invited them to the party, to get on their good side. Or maybe they didn't dare complain, because she'd already appeared in a movie and was sort of famous. People are dumb enough to do that, especially neighbors. Anyway, I looked for the Fermat name on the intercom, and rang the buzzer, which sounded staticky. I waited. I have to admit I felt nervous as I waited, because I hardly knew anybody at this party. There'd be nothing but seniors and movie actors there. In one way, I didn't give a damn, since I was coming for Mathilde, not for them, but still . . . Anyway, Marco would be there. I wouldn't be all alone, so it was no problem. I pressed the buzzer again.

"Yeah, hello. Who is it?"

A woman's voice. It must be Emilie. Shit. I'd have preferred it to be someone else, because I didn't like Emilie that much. I swallowed, then gave my name.

"It's Julien."

". . ."

"Julien Parme."

"Who?"

"Julien Parme."

"Julien Parme? Who's that?"

"Parme. Marco's friend."

"Huh?"

"Marco's friend. And Mathilde's."

"Oh yeah . . . Sixth floor."

"You mean the sixth floor upstairs?" I asked, to lighten the mood.

"What?"

"The sixth what? Upstairs?"

She wasn't getting the humor of the thing.

"Are you stupid, or what? It's not level six in the basement," she answered in a really sharp voice before pressing her button.

I'd sort of blown my introduction, but the main thing was that she'd let me in. I took a deep breath and pushed the door open. All I had to do was to go upstairs. But then I suddenly remembered that I didn't have a present for Emilie. Damn! The fact that it was a birthday party hadn't really registered, because I hadn't really expected to come—it had just happened. I began to have second thoughts. Emilie would say I was taking advantage of the situation, and maybe she'd tell Mathilde. Shit. I had to find something . . . I looked around. Between the garbage cans and the stairwell was a door that probably led to the basement. I thought I'd go look and maybe swipe something. That was a good idea. You can sometimes find terrific things in basements. Unless of course I stole it from the Fermats' own storage area. Because if I gave Emilie something that already belonged to her it might be a bit much, especially on top of my failed joke. I tried to open the door, but it was locked. Rats! I tried to force it, but it was nothing doing. I had to come up with something else.

That's when I got my idea. First I wedged the stairway door open with the welcome mat so I'd be able to get back in. The mat was perfect: nice and stiff. No problem. Then I crossed the courtyard to one of the ground-floor windows, my heart pounding, headed for the pot of geraniums on a window ledge. It wasn't the best present in the world, I admit, but it was still a present. Besides, girls like flowers. Roses, tulips, geraniums—they're pretty much all the same. You water them and then they wilt. Emilie could put them on her own window ledge. She would understand that it wasn't a present to be taken at face value. I looked around, approached the pot, and was just about to take it when a sudden noise behind me made me jump out of my skin. I almost had a heart attack, I mean it. I walked back to the entryway. The doormat had slipped, and the door had swung shut. Shit! I raced to the ground-floor window and grabbed the flowerpot. Then I went back to the intercom. After checking to make sure nobody was behind me, I rang again. I was hoping I'd get somebody else, but no, Emilie picked up again. Damn! It's her birthday and she's got nothing better to do than answer the intercom . . .

"Yeah?"

I cleared my throat a little and scratched my nose.

"Er, it's Julien again."

"What?"

It's true that with the music blaring, you couldn't hear anything.

"It's Julien again."

"Julien who?"

"Julien Parme. Marco's friend."

"Hey, I just let you in. Didn't it work?"

I thought this was a chance to salvage the lame joke I told earlier.

"Yes, sure. But I went to level six in the basement and there wasn't anybody there."

". . ."

"Hello?"

". . ."

"Hello?"

". . ."

I could hear a voice in the distance say, "Here, go ahead. He's your pal; you two work it out. He and I can't understand each other." And suddenly Marco came to the rescue.

"Hello? What are you doing?"

"Nothing. I'm downstairs. Can you let me in?"

"Yeah. Wait a sec . . . Got it?"

A metallic ringing.

"I got it. I'm coming up."

I was relieved at the thought that I would see Marco when I got to the apartment. That would make it easier. Because at this point I felt completely at sea, let me tell you. In general, I didn't give a damn about Emilie Fermat, but it would bother me if she told her sister I was a jerk and all. Anyway, it wasn't my fault if she didn't have a sense of humor. She took herself too seriously, if you ask me. When you take yourself seriously it's always because you think you have more time to live than you actually do. I know that, because I read it somewhere.

As I was climbing the stairs, I ran into two uniformed policemen calmly coming down. I swear, I almost turned and ran. Like a reflex. Even though I knew very well that they weren't there for me. But when you're screwing up, like you're a runaway, you always feel that people on every street corner are watching you. One of the policemen said good evening and gave me the once-over. I answered in my choked-up voice, while hiding my flowerpot behind my back. I wasn't looking too cool, I swear. And it suddenly occurred to me that if my mother found out I wasn't at home anymore—like if she woke up or something—the first thing she'd do would be to phone Emilie Fermat, since she knew I'd originally planned to go to her birthday party. I could imagine the cops showing up in the middle of the party and asking if there was a Julien Parme among the young people there. The thought scared the hell out of me, and I began to feel that maybe it wasn't so smart to go to the party. But the truth is, it was mainly because I was nervous about Mathilde and all. When I got to the sixth floor, I had a final moment of hesitation about my flowerpot. All in all, Emilie wasn't the kind of person to like flowers; she was more the kind to make fun of me. And I didn't want people going around saying I was romantic and all. So I decided to leave the pot off to one side, next to the neighbor's doormat. I rang the bell. The door opened right away.

"How's it going?"

It was Marco.

"How are you?"

"It's cool. Come on in. So you were able to come after all?"

"Yeah." My being there was proof, which made me happy. Also, it took him down a notch or two.

"Did you wind up ditching that girl?"

"What girl?

"The girl you had the date with."

"Which one?"

"The one you supposedly had a date with . . ."

I couldn't tell if he believed me about the Charlotte story, because he was sort of winking as he said this. Hey, too bad for him: I was here, and there was nothing he could say.

"I didn't ditch her," I answered. "It's just that I wanted to stop by and . . . What about Mathilde?"

"What about her?"

"Is she here?"

"Yeah, why?"

Right away, I told Marco I wanted to tell him something. Something absolutely important. And private. He didn't take me too seriously, but said to follow him. We walked down a long hallway. Everybody was in the living room and in the room next to it. As I walked past the door, I could see that not many people were dancing. Most of them were sitting around talking, playing it too cool for school. Some of the guys must've been twenty, if not older. I remarked that the mood seemed strange. Marco explained that the police had shown up just before I did. Supposedly because it was late and you're not allowed to make so much noise after a certain hour, like at night. Noise ordinance, he said, with a knowing smile. The neighbors had complained. So they'd had to turn the volume all the way down, which had spoiled the mood. It was kind of too bad, especially for a birthday party. "That's dumb," I said, to give the impression that I cared, but actually I was looking all over for Mathilde. People were talking about continuing the party at a nightclub, so it wouldn't be a downer.

"Oh, really?"

Nightclubs aren't really my thing. Especially since I wasn't sure they'd let me in, because of my age. It would suck to have a bouncer say, "No, not you" in front of the others. A major embarrassment.

"Yeah. Emilie says she knows a really terrific place. We're going to take off soon."

We entered a room at the end of the hallway. The guest bedroom, I guessed, where people left their coats and all. But I chose to keep my black jacket on, the one I love. Then Marco remembered that I had something important to tell him.

"So what's going on?"

Actually, I didn't really know what I felt like telling him. If I told him straight out that my mother wanted to marry François, he wouldn't understand what I was driving at. That wasn't the right approach to take. And I didn't know how to broach the subject of Mathilde. After all, I wasn't about to blurt out that I was crazy about her. He would've made fun of me. What else? The fact that I'd just run into Madame Thomas was something else I'd have liked to tell him, even if he would never have believed me. Not to mention the fact that I'd run away from home. In short, I had a ton of things to tell him, but I didn't know quite where to begin. Just as I was about to lay all this on him, Emilie Fermat came into the room. Marco introduced us. Hello, hello. She gave me an absentminded peck on the cheek and I forgot to wish her a happy birthday. Then she told Marco that she absolutely had to show him something. He agreed, the jerk, and the two of them left without me. "Wait a second, I'm coming," I said. As she went out, Emilie switched off the light, as if she'd forgotten me, I swear. I found myself in darkness. Okay, fine, really nice.

While waiting for Marco to come back, I went to check out the living room, but from a safe distance. I was somewhat uncomfortable, but not too much. There were a lot of people, all of them older than me, but to hell with them. I made a bee-line for the table with the champagne bottles. It was real champagne, too, but the bottles were all empty. People clearly hadn't waited for me to show up to start drinking. Somebody said they were getting some more from the kitchen. Cool. While I waited, I went to sit down.

At this point, I could do a number, and launch into a huge description of this party. But I've read Balzac, the guy who wrote *L'Assommoir*, and I'm not sadistic enough to make you wade through mountains of useless details. You may not necessarily want to know everything about the party, such as how many ashtrays were on the little table to the right of my chair. In fact, you may not give a damn about the party. Besides, you weren't even invited. I'm the one who dragged you there, so I take responsibility. I'll cut it short. The only thing you need to know is that I wondered more and more what the hell I was doing there. I felt ill at ease, and minuscule. Transparent, and useless, like a flea on a bald man's head.

A blonde girl sat down next to me. She was incredibly tall, but it was okay when she was sitting down. I asked her what her name was. Maybe it was stupid, but I couldn't resist.

"Marion," she answered and turned away.

But I immediately returned to the fray. I asked if I could take a sip from her glass of champagne, because I was dying of thirst and all the bottles were empty. I know it's not the sort of thing you say, but I sensed that she hadn't touched her champagne glass for hours. Besides, she was never going to finish it. Otherwise, I wouldn't have dared. She looked at me strangely before giving a sort of funny answer: "I don't feel right about that, because then you'll be able to read my thoughts." Because of the old saying. I thought that was pretty classy. So I waited for the fresh bottles from the kitchen.

Ten minutes later, I was still in the same position and I still hadn't spoken to anyone. I was still wearing a big smile, relaxed but a little frozen, so it wouldn't be too obvious that I was uncomfortable. In any case, nobody seemed to have noticed me. I wondered where Marco was. As I lit a cigarette I told myself that I really wanted to confide in him. At the same time I couldn't see myself telling him everything about running away. I'd rather he realize that he'd been wrong about me, that I wasn't the sort to be punished by my mother, and so on. But even as I was thinking that, I also thought the opposite. He might be able to give me some advice about what to do now. For example, where was I going to sleep tonight? My first thought was to go to his place, obviously. It was strange in a way, because I'd spent all evening hating him because of the trick he'd pulled about Mathilde. But now I'd almost forgotten that, because all that mattered right then was telling him how I'd run away from home. I needed to. In fact, I think I was feeling a little lost. On the one hand I was definitely happy to be at the party, but on the other, I had a feeling I was going to regret it.

From what I understood, my mother had asked my uncle in Nice if he could take me in, and he'd said no. I understood that. Problem was, he was all the family I had. My mother didn't have a brother or parents anymore. She'd apparently had a brother once, but he died in an accident when they were little. She never talked about it. After that I lost both my grandmothers. Really lousy luck. On my father's side there was my uncle, but he didn't have any children. So basically, if I left my mother I'd wind up with no family at all. I felt lonely, and it made my stomach hurt, as if I had swallowed a nail. I enjoyed being with Marco, even if he wasn't family. He was reassuring, in a way. Because Marco was far from stupid. Even though he came close sometimes.

But he wasn't coming back, and Mathilde was still nowhere to be seen. More and more, I wondered if coming here hadn't been the biggest mistake of my life. I looked around. Honestly, there was nothing very fascinating going on. This party of theirs wasn't exactly the big time. True, there was champagne and all, but . . . I don't know. The people all looked stupid and self-satisfied. Plus, I was afraid the cops would suddenly show up, I swear. I couldn't get that idea out of my head. They would handcuff me and all. I hoped that at least Mathilde would see that. Maybe it would be best if I left right away. With the money from François's credit card, I could do whatever I wanted. Why did I have to stay at this party? I was sure all sorts of fascinating things happened in Paris at night. All you had to do was to walk around and bump into the right people. What I would've liked would be to have incredible adventures. I hadn't really thought it through, but with the money I could even buy a train ticket and go way the hell far away. To Italy, for example. With Marco. We could leave in the morning, after stopping by the bank to withdraw the max. We'd treat ourselves to a whole month of peace and happiness, instead of going to stupid parties with self-satisfied jerks. The idea cheered me up. It wasn't just tonight that was ahead of me, it was all of life. I wanted a drink to celebrate that. Because people were still waiting for the famous bottles from the kitchen, and also just for fun, I went back to my blonde neighbor.

"What are you thinking about?" I asked.

Marion was wearing the same vacant look as before.

"What?"

"What are you thinking about?"

"Nothing," she answered, a little surprised by my question.

"In that case, I can have a drink from your glass."

First she looked at me as if I'd just landed from another planet, then she laughed. I'd said it seriously, but she thought I was being witty. In connection with what she'd told me the first time.

"What's your name?"

"Julien."

"You a friend of Emilie's?"

"More or less."

"How old are you?"

That question annoyed me, just then.

"I'm sixteen. Why?"

"No reason."

She stood up—Mount Everest—and held her glass out to me. "Here, go ahead. I'm finished." She left the living room and headed toward the bedrooms. I downed all her champagne.

As I drank it, I mulled over the idea of asking Marco to let me crash at his place for the night. His bedroom was big enough for both of us, but it was risky. It would be the first place my mother would come looking for me in the morning. When she woke up and saw I hadn't slept at home, she'd head straight for Marco's, to find out where I was hiding. No doubt about that.

So it was no dice. What would've been good would be if my father were still alive, I thought as I finished the glass. I'd go to his place and tell him I'd had a fight with my mother. He would've understood, since in those days he did nothing but fight with her. He would've approved. And I'd be able to sleep at his place. All right, maybe he would've chewed me out for leaving home in the middle of the night, but in a nice way, just enough so I didn't do it again. Maybe I could've even gone to live with him in his apartment for good. That's where I would've written my novel. He knew literature really well since he'd been a journalist before. Being a journalist and a writer is practically the same job. Not really the same, since they're exactly the opposite, but almost. In any case, if he'd been alive, my father would've been happy to know I was writing books.

Marco finally came back to the living room. I went right over to him.

"What the hell have you been up to?"

"Tell you later," he answered mysteriously.

"Go on, tell me now."

"I've got something going."

"A girl?"

"Yeah. A real hottie."

I was intrigued, of course. "Come here, I'll show her to you." Marco took me by the arm and led me toward the kitchen. He looked really excited. Was he referring to Mathilde? Along the way, he shook hands with three guys who acted as if I wasn't there.

"Do you know who that was?" he asked me after exchanging a few words with one of them.

"Who?"

"The guy I just spoke to."

"No. Who was it?"

He said a name I didn't know and I've since forgotten. I think it was an actor from Emilie Fermat's movie—another someone who thought he was famous. But when someone is famous but nobody knows it, they're just not famous, that's all. Logical, right? But I hypocritically raised my eyebrows to show how impressed I was. Marco looked pleased that I'd seen him talk with a guy I was pretending to know. It made him happy.

"Here, it's this way."

He was leading me around like it was his own place.

"Their apartment's huge."

"You didn't know? It's their father's."

"Their parents are divorced?"

"Well, yeah. Like everybody."

He could talk. Not only were his parents still together, but in addition they lived in Morocco. Supposedly.

"So where are we going?"

"You'll see."

We stopped at the end of the hallway. He knocked on a door and we went into the bathroom. A guy and two girls had gone in there, to get some peace and quiet. The bathtub was full of ice, to keep the bottles cold. It was where the bottles were stashed.

"What d'you want?" asked the guy.

One of the girls, a brunette, was wearing a top so sheer you could clearly see her nipples through it. She was Marco's target, no doubt about that.

"Go ahead, pop the champagne."

He sent a cork flying.

"In the living room they're all waiting for fresh bottles," I said.

That cracked everyone up, even though there was nothing funny about it. I was just informing them. But the information cracked them up. Don't ask me why. Anyway, that's when I got a shock. The guy across from me was the spitting image of Yann Chevillard, but I couldn't tell if it was really him or not. Yann Chevillard was a guy I'd wanted to catch up with for years so I could beat the shit out of him for all the dirty tricks he pulled on me. I'll tell you about them sometime. In the meantime, we were short a glass. I said I'd go get one, so I left the bathroom, still with the uneasy feeling that maybe I'd found that scumbag Chevillard. As I walked down the long hallway toward the living room I finally saw Mathilde. She wasn't in the living room but in the room next to it, looking to pour herself a glass of champagne. It made me really nervous, like seeing an apparition. I wanted to shift into reverse, or hide. But at the same time, I was here to see her. This was no time to chicken out; just the opposite. Especially since it might be the last time I would see her, given my situation. I went over and stood next to her. It took her at least a minute to notice me.

"Hey, hello there," she said to me.

"Hi."

Without meaning to, I had answered really coldly.

"They're empty," I added, pointing to the bottles, in an attempt to relax the mood.

She smiled at me, and moved away. Shit. I took a swallow from my empty glass, to give myself time to come up with another idea. With all the liquor I had drunk, I was beginning to lose it a little. Mathilde went to sit by herself near the window. After all, she didn't know anybody here either, I told myself. It was her sister's birthday, not hers. She seemed as bored as I was. Looking at her on the window ledge like that, it occurred to me that she was the opposite of her sister. Those two had nothing in common. You wouldn't have thought they came out of the same belly. If you ask me, it was strange how they didn't look at all like each other, for two sisters. Especially Mathilde.

I headed back to the bathroom with my glass. Once there, Marco filled it to the brim. We clinked glasses. The brunette's nipples were still sticking up. As if she was doing it on purpose, to turn you on. A cock tease, in other words. I probed the guy I had taken for Yann Chevillard. "It's amazing how much you look like a guy I used to know," I said, without specifying that the guy in question was the biggest asshole who ever walked the Earth. Then I said I'd be right back, took the bottle, and headed for the living room with the idea of pouring Mathilde a glass. She was still in the same place by the window. I went to sit down next to her. Feeling nervous, of course. I offered her some champagne. She held out her glass. Then she said thank you. And then we couldn't think of anything else to say.

We sat in silence like that for quite a long time. I pretended to be looking around or reading the label on the bottle. A few people continued dancing, even though the music had been turned down low. I wondered if they were really having fun or just showing off. I think they were just showing off. People love to pretend that they're enjoying themselves.

Several minutes dragged by in slow motion while thousands of sentences crowded my mind in every direction, as I searched for something to say to her. Then I jumped in with both feet.

"The music isn't bad, is it?"

"You think so? I don't much like it."

"Yeah, actually, that's true, the music isn't terrific. It's like what they play on the radio."

I let a moment go by while I considered adding, "You're right, this music is really lousy. I've listened to it carefully. It's stupid." But I decided to move on to another subject, so as not to seem wishy-washy.

"In any case, as far as the mood goes . . ."

"What?"

"I was saying as far as the mood goes . . ."

". . ."

I looked around.

"You get the impression they're pretending to have fun."

"Who?"

"Well—them," I answered, pointing to the two people dancing right in front of us.

"You think so?"

"I don't know."

She looked at me with her beautiful green eyes. Oh man . . . I felt that everything I was saying was stupid. But I didn't know what else to say, so I took another swallow of my champagne. I usually do pretty well with girls. By that I mean I don't spend hours beating around the bush. I play it seductive, and sometimes it works. That doesn't mean that I get all that far every time. It depends on the girl. With some girls it's impossible to get very far no matter what. Even if you're perfect, witty, and with a feeling for poetry and all, some of them brush you off on principle, and from my point of view that's really painful. But being there with Mathilde was different. What I had in mind wasn't just flirting with her. I can tell you now that with Mathilde, it was love—the genuine article.

"Lucky we don't have class tomorrow," I said, to keep the silence from lasting too long.

"Yeah."

"We would've been wasted."

"Uh-huh."

When silence lasts a long time, it gets oppressive. You get the feeling that everybody can hear what's going through your mind.

"So if I understand right, this is your father's place."

"Yeah. Well, his and his girlfriend's."

"Oh, he has a girlfriend?"

Then she told me that her father was living with a really young girl. Not as young as us, of course, but still. From my point of view that would have been weird. But Mathilde didn't say anything about it. The only thing that bothered her was that she didn't get along with the girl at all. Anyway, she didn't care that much. She went to her father's as little as possible. Sometimes just for the weekend. Then I asked her what a teacher training day was. She pursed her lips, surprised at the way I was stringing my questions together. It's true that they weren't connected with each other. It's just that while she was answering one question, I was thinking about the next one, so of course I couldn't always catch exactly what she was saying. For some reason, I started thinking about my mother just then. Though there was really no connection there, either. It occurred to me that even if it hadn't been a teacher training day, I still couldn't have gone to class the next morning. For strategic reasons. Because if I'd gone, my mother would've found me right away. Going to class the day after running away, that was jumping into the lion's den. And in that case I'd be off to Les Roches Noires come Monday morning, let me tell you. So I couldn't go back to school—not Saturday, not Monday, not ever. It would be like going to the police station to confess and supplying your own handcuffs. I was starting to realize that there were actually lots of places I now had to avoid. Okay. All that stuff was running through my mind. I should have kept it to myself, like a treasure, instead of blurting everything out to Mathilde like a burst balloon.

"Anyway, I think I'm going to be having a whole week of teacher training days."

She laughed. I enjoyed that. With girls, humor can pay off big time.

"What do you mean?" she finally asked.

"Well, I probably won't be going to class. Not even on Monday."

"Oh?"

"Yeah."

"Why?"

"I've been having problems with my mother. Turns out I may be leaving the Institut."

Her face suddenly changed.

"Is that true?"

"Yeah, maybe."

"Oh, really? What happened with your mother?"

"It's too complicated to explain. Let's say that we never got along very well, her and I. So now I may have to go live somewhere else."

She opened her eyes wide. They were usually half closed, but here, she really opened them. I sensed that the conversation interested her.

"At your father's?" she asked.

"No, I can't. He's dead."

It was the first time I'd said it like that. On that question, I usually manage to change the subject, don't ask me why. But there, maybe because of the liquor and also because of what I felt for her, I told Mathilde everything.

"Was it a long time ago?"

"When I was nine. He had cancer."

She looked at me without saying anything. That whole period is pretty fuzzy in my mind, actually. First, because I was small, but also because I didn't think about it very often. All I knew is that my parents separated because they fought all the time, and then my father suddenly got sick. It all happened very fast. We hardly had time to turn around. The memories I have of that time, just before his illness, were that I went to his place every weekend. He'd rented an apartment in the same neighborhood as us. I went to see him and I slept on the living room sofa bed. I remember that clearly, even though it was five years ago. In the evening we often watched videos. His TV was even bigger than ours at home. But aside from that, I don't quite remember what we did together. He looked really depressed about not living with my mother anymore, probably because he still loved her. I even saw him cry once. That was a shock, let me tell you. A father should never cry, if you ask me. But he couldn't help it, he was too sad. My parents didn't get along. Between the two of them, it was nonstop screaming. I swear. So it was better that they each lived in their own apartment. Even if it made my father sad. But that's when he got sick. Right after their separation. I'd say six months afterward, something like that. After that, it went like lightning. And that took us directly to the day of his funeral, when the weather was strangely beautiful. My mother wore sunglasses.

That's about all I know.

"What about your parents?" I asked, so as not to monopolize the conversation.

She told me that they'd been divorced for quite some time, but that she thought that it was just as well that way. The worst, according to her, were people who fought for years without ever having the courage to separate. In some ways I agreed with her, but in my opinion it didn't happen all that often. Her sister got along better with their father. Seeing as how he also worked in movies. He was a producer, and that was how Emilie had been able to make her first movie. I was starting to understand the ins and outs of the situation. Mathilde, on the other hand, was closer to her mother. In short, she was telling me about her life. It was really interesting. But she could've told me boring stuff and I'd still be perfectly happy. Then she asked me what I wanted to do. "In life?" I asked. I thought it strange to have a girl ask you what you wanted to do in life. It occurred to me that that might be a bad sign. As if we didn't have a lot to talk about. When you don't have a lot to talk about, you can always fall back on the kinds of subjects that work with everybody. Anyway, I acted as if nothing was wrong. I don't know if you've noticed, but the job everybody wants today is to be an actor or a singer. I told her I'd rather be a writer. I felt stupid and pretentious the moment I admitted that, but it was the truth, though. For once I wasn't bullshitting. But anyway it's not the sort of thing that you say. It's showing off. So she asked me what I was writing. And to make things worse, I answered, "A novel."

"Do you have a title already?"

My thoughts raced for a fraction of a second, and I said the first thing that came to mind.

"Yeah. *Death in Denise*," I answered. "But it's a temporary title."

I had to explain that Denise Morozvitch had been my former neighbor, and almost my grandmother, see. We spent a fair amount of time together until her son shipped her off to an old folks home. My story was about that. And while I was telling her this stuff, I was thinking that it was actually a really good idea. Mathilde repeated my title aloud, as if to appraise it: "Death in Denise." I was afraid of what she was going to say. Maybe she thought it was a lousy title, or . . . I don't know. In any case, to avoid that, I decided to change the subject as fast as possible.

"So you know Marco well," I said.

"Yeah."

That chilled me. She said it as if it was obvious.

"How come?"

"Oh, I don't know. He's a friend of my sister's. They were in the same class a long time ago. And we live really close, two blocks away. That's why. I don't know him that well."

While we were talking, most of the people were getting ready to leave. We didn't know if they were going home, or if they were going to the nightclub in question to wrap up the evening. Anyway, we had finished our glasses. The bottle I had brought was empty. Not because we'd been drinking like fishes, but because it was practically empty when I brought it. Mathilde was thirsty. I told her we could find drinks in the bathroom. We stood up and walked down the hallway. But inside the bathroom there was only the brunette, who was smoking a very thin cigarette. She asked me where Marco was. I told her I didn't know. "You can tell him that I'm waiting for him here," she said. At that Mathilde, give a cute little laugh. Then, as we were walking past the door to her bedroom, she gestured to me, meaning, "Come and see." She apparently wanted to show me something. I followed her without saying anything. I swear, into her bedroom where she sleeps and all. She closed the door behind us. I couldn't believe it. And that's when I learned something that floored me.

Chapter 11

It was an ordinary bedroom except for the walls, which were covered with posters of horses. No kidding—just like Bénédicte's. Mathilde looked at a clock above her desk. It was nearly 2 a.m.

"Do you ride?" I asked casually, in spite of my embarrassment and surprise.

"Yes. Every week."

"Oh? That's . . . cool."

"I love it."

All right. At this point I have to admit I sort of changed my tune.

"So do I."

"You ride too?"

"Yeah. Riding's my thing."

Damn! I could just imagine what Bénédicte would say if she heard me. I'd never hear the end of it. Because I used to say she was just "horsing around" all the time, to piss her off. It usually infuriated her. She would chase me around the apartment, trying to hit me with her riding crop. Life really is strange.

"Where do you ride?" Mathilde asked.

For the life of me, I couldn't remember the name of my future stepsister's riding club. I decided to duck the issue.

"Actually I mainly ride during vacations. I have an uncle who lives near Nice. He's got a meadow."

"Oh?"

"Yeah. It's handy for grazing."

The truth is, I'd never tried to get onto a horse.

"What about you?" I asked.

"Every Saturday. In the Bois de Boulogne."

"Boulogne is handy too, compared to Nice."

I looked at the posters again. Mathilde must have sensed that I thought it odd for a girl to put up things like that. As if to justify herself, she told me something I already knew, namely that this wasn't really her bedroom, since she lived somewhere else during the week. She came to her father's as rarely as possible, so she hadn't actually decorated her room in this apartment. I felt relieved anyway.

Then she gestured to me again. No doubt about it, hand gestures were Mathilde's thing. I came closer. She opened the window.

"Look."

Because we were up so high, the view was terrific. Off to the side was the Eiffel Tower, whose lights were already out. The Musée d'Orsay was a little further to the left, and the Seine

JULIEN PARME · 131

snaked off into the distance. Everything was sunk in the deepest slumber. It was pretty amazing to have a view like that from her bedroom, all to herself.

"It's wild," I remarked.

Then the window across the way caught my eye, because it was the only one still lit up. Mathilde smiled to let me know that this was actually what she wanted to show me. Just this window in the middle of the darkness. A smile was all it took. The sight intrigued me. Because of the light, it was like a window onto another world. It sort of looked like a library, or rather a study. In any case, there was a wooden table with books everywhere, and a globe.

"That window is always lit up at night."

"Why?"

"That's just it, I don't know. I wonder . . . The lights are on every night, but there's never anybody there."

"That's strange."

"It's something I'd like to understand."

We spent a long time looking at it. Wondering what could go on in that room at night. It was like an enigma. The study was just a few yards away, in spite of the drop and the six floors. You felt you could reach out your hand and practically touch it. It was a nice feeling. We were standing side by side, our shoulders touching, and it was as silent as a church. A slight breeze played in Mathilde's hair. I could hear her breathing. I was right there, yet I also wasn't there, at her bedroom window. I was across the way, in that empty study. And I was thinking that it must be a writer's study, and that was why she'd wanted to show it to me. Since I'd told her that's what I wanted to be, a writer. Then it occurred to me that she must look at that study often. Maybe every night before going to sleep when she was at her father's. And that every time, she wondered why it was both lit up and empty. Every evening, the same mystery. And the little wind in her hair. Yeah, that was it, I told myself. I imagined her standing at her window. Mathilde, all dreamy and everything. I was really moved that she'd asked me to look with her, just this evening. And that without even speaking, we could both wonder why the study was lit up though nobody seemed to be writing in it. Words had become unnecessary. There was nothing to say, except that it was wonderful. But we didn't even need to say that, because we understood each other. The sight spoke for itself. All we had to do was to remain silent in the face of this mystery. The way you feel whenever something important is happening. I felt moved. I was shivering, there at her bedroom window. Because I understood perfectly that what she'd suggested looking at with her was something really rare and precious. And that nothing could spoil the power of this instant. That's what I told myself. At this instant, the world could crumble. No kidding, it could disappear. I was ready. Everything will disappear someday, anyway. Everything will change. There's nothing we can do about it, that's the way it is. But there's one thing that won't ever change, I told myself. One thing will survive the destruction of the world, the joy of having been with her. At this precise place. At this precise instant.

Mathilde was really an unusual girl. If I'd dared, that's what I would have told her, but I didn't dare, so I didn't say anything. But even if I'd dared, I wouldn't have had the time anyway, since someone was knocking on the door. She looked at me as if it was time to say good-bye. I was really touched by that. Then she went to open the door. It was Marco from Morocco, followed by the brunette with the stiff nipples.

"Oh there you are! What are you doing?" he asked Mathilde.

"Huh? Nothing."

Then, after glancing at me, she added, "We were talking."

"So? We're the last ones here. They've all gone downstairs already."

Mathilde said she wasn't coming with us. I'd noticed that she didn't actually like her sister's friends that much. I would've been happy to stay with her, but nobody suggested it. I had no idea what I was going to do. On the one hand, I didn't want to wind up all alone. But on the other, I was afraid of not being able to get into their nightclub. And once inside, I was sure to be bored out of my skull. Since I don't dance. To hear Marco tell it, the neighborhood was teeming with nightclubs. You didn't have to go all the way to Alsace for one. You could just walk a few steps in any direction. But Emilie absolutely wanted to go to some place near Bastille. Don't ask me why. Anyway, we were supposed to take a taxi. Maybe several taxis, since there were a lot of us.

"All right. Let's get going . . ."

Marco turned to Mathilde to give her a kiss good-bye. Just then we heard a very deep voice in the hallway. It was her father. We left the room, trying to look innocent. She introduced us. The guy was pretty impressive. Very dark hair. He didn't seem to be in a very good mood. We understood that it was time for us to beat it. Mathilde accompanied us to the front door.

"All right then. So long," I said.

"So long."

That was pretty cold, because of the presence of Marco and the girl, whose name was Alice. Mathilde just smiled a little. It broke my heart, since I didn't know when I'd see her again. But at the same time, I felt good. Because the moment we had shared together at her window was a really great moment.

"See you soon," I added.

She opened the front door.

Just then, Marco realized he had forgotten his jacket and ran to the back bedroom. I figured he was going to bump into Mathilde's father, and feel really awkward. The rest of us stood around in front of the open door, not saying anything in particular. I felt the pressure. Several times I thought of walking over to Mathilde and kissing her, but that scared me too much, even though I thought it was stupid to be scared about a kiss. Having Alice there rattled me. To kiss a girl, the circumstances have to be just right. I'll count to three, I told myself, and then I'll do it. But at three I started at zero again. So I let the opportunity slip by, and Marco came back.

"You sure you don't want to come along?"

"Yeah, yeah."

"Too bad. All right, so long."

First Marco kissed her goodnight, then Alice did, then I did. And our lips touched a little bit, right at the corners. Just a little. I was struck dumb. But I didn't know if I had dreamed it. Or if it meant anything. At the time, I certainly believed so. Not a kiss, no. But almost. Mathilde gave me an odd smile. And the door closed on us. I didn't know what to think anymore, except that I was happy. At least I think I was.

Chapter 12

Emilie's gang was supposed to wait for us out on the sidewalk on rue Pierre-Charron, but when we got downstairs, there wasn't anybody left. Everyone had already taken off. Marco went nuts. It bugged him that Alice and I were witnessing this. If you ask me, he was so full of himself that any little snag was enough to make him sick. He took out his cell phone and said he would fix everything, but he just got voicemail. You could have seen that one coming. He tried some other numbers, but struck out again. The others had had a little too much to drink, and they'd completely blown us off. So there we were on the sidewalk, like idiots. A bad plan, and all. I wasn't paying too much attention to any of that, though. I was busy trying to spot the Fermats' window, but you couldn't actually see it from where we were, since their apartment faced the inner courtyard.

From what I gathered, Alice was a childhood friend of Emilie's, and they knew each other well. But when Alice phoned, she got voicemail too. At that, I suggested we go have a drink. It wasn't a fantastic suggestion, but after all, there was nothing else we could do. The two of them had left messages, and they figured the others would call us right back. There was no point standing around outside in the meantime. Especially because I was worried that everybody would go home and I'd wind up alone. So we cut over toward the Champs. Oddly enough, we didn't see a soul, not even at the taxi stand. You could tell Marco was feeling a little fed up. In fact I'm sure he was wondering if they hadn't ditched us on purpose. From my point of view, it was all to the good. I really didn't feel like spending the night with jerks. So I started trashing them, to cheer him up. Within three minutes Marco had come around to my way of thinking, namely that everyone in Emilie's gang was a real loser. Even the girls.

We walked up the avenue toward the Arc de Triomphe. Alice kept hobbling after us in her high heels and yelling, "Wait for me!" and we kept waiting for her. At one point I told Marco I had to get some money. I went to a cash machine and withdrew a whole thousand euros. I swear. That was the maximum the machine would cough up. Otherwise, I would've taken like ten thousand. I stuffed the wad into my breast pocket. It gave me a funny feeing, sort of like the day of my first communion. I told Marco we were good to go. He'd been too busy checking out Alice's cleavage and hadn't noticed a thing. I was really pleased with my trick. I was looking forward to seeing his face when I showed him all the money.

But at the same time, I was on edge. The Champs was sort of scary. At this time of night, it was crawling with lowlifes.

Besides, Marco had started to tell us a hair-raising story. A friend of his mother's was withdrawing money on the Champs once—in the middle of the night, as it happens. And suddenly he feels the cold barrel of a gun on his neck. I swear, right on his neck. And this isn't Paraguay! This is France, I'm telling you! The guy tells him to get into his car, which is parked nearby. Marco's mother's friend can't do a thing. If he doesn't get into the car, the guy'll blow his brains out. So he's in a really shitty situation. With a hopped-up, whacked-out nut case driving at top speed and telling him to shut up when he asks where he's being taken. The guy with the gun says he doesn't want to hear Marco's mother's friend's voice. If he hears his voice once more, it'll be the last time, because he'll waste him in a flash. So the friend keeps quiet for the whole trip, even though it lasts more than half an hour. They head out toward the suburbs. The guy with the gun must have been out of his gourd, according to Marco, because he was super nervous and everything. Anyway, after a horrible half hour, the guy tells him to get out of the car. They've arrived. At a kind of vacant lot in the middle of nowhere. This is it. Marco's mother's friend really thinks he's going to be whacked. Why else take him to this vacant lot? He begs, but it's nothing doing. The guy tells him to kneel down in the middle of the field with his hands on his head, and to stop bawling like a girl. They're waiting for somebody, is what the guy with the gun tells him. They're waiting for two of his pals. To do what? Nobody knows. Not very nice things, that's for sure.

They wait, but the two guys they're waiting for don't show up. That makes the guy with the gun even more jumpy, waiting in the cold for guys who aren't coming. Plus now he's talking to himself, saying incomprehensible stuff. A wacko, in other words. And high, too. Marco's mother's friend is trembling, he's afraid he'll piss his pants, he's saying his prayers. This lasts at least a half hour. Complete torture. But in the end, the guy tells him to stand up and to get out of there. "Go on, beat it," he says. The truth is, he's tired of waiting. He understands that his pals aren't coming. The guy doesn't even take the man's wallet. Like it wasn't for money at all that he did it. What for, then? Marco's mother's friend wondered afterward. Today, though, he's just as happy not knowing. There are things you'd rather never know your whole life. In any case, it sends a chill down your back, when you think of it.

"Why are you telling us this?" I asked him, picking up the pace a little, but discreetly.

"No reason."

No reason. That killed me.

A few dozen yards further on, we turned right into a little street that was still lit up. Marco supposedly knew a kind of pub there. It was one of the last places in the neighborhood still open. Otherwise we would've had to go to a nightclub. But Marco and I didn't really feel like it. We just wanted to sit down at a table and have a friendly drink. When we opened the door, the music grabbed us by the throat. The place was jumping. We went to sit at a table. A girl came right over to us. I swear, but she was just a waitress. Marco wanted to order beers, like a small-time operator. So I interrupted him, acting sure of myself and all, and said:

"Champagne!"

"Three glasses?" asked the waitress, just to be sure.

"No, no," I corrected her right away. "The whole bottle!"

She looked surprised. So did Marco.

"My treat," I said.

The girl waited for Marco's reaction, as if everything depended on his opinion and he was the one to decide. What a cow. He said okay, and she finally left us in peace. Most waitresses are cows. Serving drinks to just anybody, they don't know a thing about life. Especially since beer is fine when you're fourteen, but it doesn't cut it after that. You have to move on to something else. Champagne is cool. That's what I told Marco, in fact: "Champagne is cool!" But he couldn't hear; we weren't able to talk over the music. To say something, you had to scream, so I screamed again: "Better to keep drinking champagne!"

I looked around. There were almost no girls in the bar, just guys. You wondered what hole they'd crawled out of. Dressed like yokels, and all. The kind of people who drink beer, if you know what I mean. In short, a pretty mediocre place. Alice was looking around, wide-eyed. You could feel she was wondering what the hell she was doing there, with the two of us. Though when I think back on everything that happened later, I can say that this was still a good time, in the pub. It was later that things went downhill.

The girl brought us the bottle, with everybody watching. First class, right this way. Just the same, she asked me to pay right away, so we wouldn't run out without paying, which must happen sometimes. But that didn't bother me, since paying under Marco's nose was what I'd been waiting to do for the last ten minutes. So I pulled out a hundred-euro note, just like that. But she took it without batting an eye, like it happened every day. So to impress her, I added:

"Keep the change."

It was like being in the movies. I couldn't get over it. Neither could Marco. He was blown away. Actually, we were both blown away. It was really something. Then Alice stood up to go to the bathroom, leaving the two of us alone, just us men. Marco was going on and on about the tip. To let him know that I could afford it, I showed him my wad, but really discreetly. It killed him on the spot.

"Son of a bitch! Where'd you get all that?"

"In Morocco," I answered, to annoy him.

I must say, I was feeling great because of Mathilde, even though I couldn't tell if I was kidding myself about the kiss business. Sometimes there are things where you don't know if they actually happened or if you made them up, just because you really want them to be true. But I was certainly feeling something intense inside.

"So how do you like her?" Marco asked

"Mathilde?"

"No, of course not. Alice."

"I don't know."

"Problem is, she already has a boyfriend, see. And she seems to be stuck on him. I spent the whole evening trying stuff, but . . ."

I wasn't listening to him anymore. I was somewhere else. I was thinking back to the business with the kiss. I don't think our lips actually touched. But almost.

"Are you listening to me? What are you thinking about?"

Marco was starting to get nasty. I'm sure it was because he was irritated at being ditched by the others. And also by Alice, who apparently wouldn't kiss him. And now I was blowing him off as well, though in a nice way, by not listening to him. He was like a washed-up singer losing his audience. Marco was the kind who always had to be the center of attention. That sort of guy kills me. But now he was getting more aggressive, whereas it should have been me. He went back to my story about Charlotte, the girl I'd pretended to have a date with, and said I'd been bullshitting him. Then he started in on Mathilde, and that was much less funny. He went on and on because he'd caught us, her and me, talking in her bedroom. But from the way he was talking, I got the strong impression that he'd already gone out with her and was glad to let me have her. Because she was fourteen years old going on twelve, he said. I couldn't believe it.

"That's stupid," I counterattacked. "Mathilde isn't my type at all."

The fact was, I really didn't want him to get involved in any of that stuff.

"Oh yeah?"

"Yeah, not at all."

"So what's your type?"

"My type of girl?"

"Yeah. What's your type of girl?"

I looked around to find an example, but there were just guys in the bar, no girls, except for the waitress, and she was a cow. I shrugged. Marco was laughing, making fun of me, and it drove me nuts. I poured two more glasses of champagne, to give myself time to come up with something. Then I asked to see his cell phone. At first, it was just to calm him down. I didn't at all anticipate what would happen next. He was sort of amused, and handed it to me, without understanding. I showed him the number on the screen, his last incoming call, and said:

"See that? That's the number of the girl who's my type."

"Oh, yeah?"

He didn't believe me. So I rolled out the big guns.

"You know her, for that matter. In fact, you know her very well."

"Who is it?"

"Madame Thomas."

It took him a moment to grasp what I was saying.

"Yeah, sure!" he finally said.

"I'm telling you."

"Oh, cut it out . . ."

"I was with her when I called earlier. Before I came to the party."

"You think I'm an idiot, or something?"

"Charlotte is Madame Thomas's first name. Her name is Charlotte Thomas."

Now Marco was looking sort of strange. He and I had often talked about Madame Thomas. To him, she was a perfect 10.

"You want me to believe that the Charlotte you were talking about earlier, the one you supposedly had a date with, is the French teacher?"

"I didn't want to tell you at first, but now that you've got her number, I have to let you in on the secret."

"Yeah, whatever."

"But promise you won't tell anyone."

"Tell what? That you're sleeping with the teacher?"

"It's really important for you to keep quiet about it, because she's married, and the thing between her and me, see, it's totally clandestine."

I was getting carried away.

"Yeah, sure."

"Especially because she may be pregnant."

He started laughing again, as if I had told him a joke. That really pissed me off. For once I was telling him the truth!

"You don't believe me?"

"No."

"You don't believe me?"

"I just told you, no."

I thought for a second. Just then, Alice came back from the bathroom. She drained her glass and looked at us curiously, as if she was trying to figure out what we were talking about, but at the same time she really didn't care.

"All right, go ahead, and call that number," I said. "You'll see who you get."

"Sure . . ."

"Go on, go ahead. Just ask to speak to Julien Parme. She'll understand, since I called on her cell earlier. You'll see."

"But it's really late . . ."

"See, you're chickening out."

"No I'm not . . ."

He glanced at Alice, who shrugged, because she didn't understand a thing, except that a sort of challenge was involved. She was probably thinking we were ten years old. So Marco pressed the redial button. Suddenly, he looked nervous. He wasn't acting so smart anymore. And he hadn't seen anything yet. Me, I was having a ball.

"It's ringing . . ."

"Of course it's ringing."

We waited for a moment.

"Who are you calling?" asked Alice.

We were concentrating so hard that neither of us answered her.

"Ah, the voicemail . . ." Marco reported, feeling relieved.

He listened to the outgoing message. Suddenly, he turned pale. He'd just understood whose message it was: Madame Thomas's.

"Son of a bitch! It was her!"

The guy couldn't believe it.

"Of course it was her."

"Who?" Alice asked again.

For at least ten seconds, Marco looked dazed; then he went on with the conversation. "But what were you guys doing?"

"What do you think?" I looked up at the ceiling, as if it were obvious.

"When you called me, you were with her?"

"Yeah. We were at her place. In her bedroom, if you must know. Afterward, I wanted to come see you. But just between the two of us, you sort of oversold the party a little. This champagne isn't bad, is it?"

You should have seen his face.

"I can't believe it . . ."

"What are you talking about?"

"It's unbelievable . . . He's getting it on with one of our teachers . . . I just had her on the phone. I can't believe it . . . He's getting it on with the French teacher!"

I didn't say anything else. I got up to go take a piss, leaving Marco there like an awestruck pygmy. He was just sitting there with Alice, shattered.

When I came back, Marco was where I'd left him. He was looking blank. Alice was talking to him, but I could tell he wasn't listening. In fact I had barely sat down when he started bombarding me with questions. How had I gone about it? What was she like in bed? How long had it been? He wanted to know everything, in other words. But I deliberately dodged the questions, just to drive him crazy.

"But who is this teacher you're talking about?" asked Alice.

Then closing time came. I didn't know bars closed so early. It must've been around three in the morning, maybe four. And the others still hadn't called us back. Too bad; we weren't about to beg them. But it bugged me that the bar was closing already. I would've liked to stay until dawn. But no, it was impossible. Like a bathtub, the room gradually emptied out, and we wound up high, dry, and naked. Pretty chilly. We understood that it was time to leave. And that's how we wound up in the street.

"Okay. Where are you heading?" asked Marco, yawning.

The fateful question.

"What about you? You taking a cab?"

"I dunno . . ."

"I am. I'll drop you off, if you want."

I was playing the big shot. But I mainly didn't feel like being alone in this neighborhood. The story Marco told about the guy being mugged wasn't the sort of thing to make you too trusting. Insecurity exists. Ever since I'd gotten the money from the cash machine, I'd been acting like a rich guy. At the next elections, I could almost have voted for the right, if I'd been old enough to vote. Which would have been really something, since I'm usually more for the other side—for equality, I mean. And to my mind, the worst inequality of all is that the people who need money most are always the ones who have the least.

We didn't have to wait for long. A taxi stopped in front of us on the Champs right away, and a moment later, the three of us were driving through the dark streets of Paris. Marco wasn't saying anything anymore. I didn't know if it was because he was worn out or because he was jealous. If you ask me, he couldn't get my business with Madame Thomas out of his head. As a result, he was completely neglecting Alice. As for me, I was dreading the moment when we would get to his place. Once we were there, I wouldn't know what to do next. A shiver went through me. I checked my pack of cigarettes: I still had about a dozen left. I hadn't smoked much all evening, actually. Fine. I could always smoke. It's not true that a dog is man's best friend. Man's best friend is a cigarette. But come on, I wasn't going to spend the rest of the night chain smoking. What else could I do? I wasn't able to think. My thoughts were getting mixed up. When I closed my eyes, my head spun. I'd had too much to drink.

Meanwhile, Alice was making conversation all by herself. The end of the evening with us must have been real unpleasant, but she seemed to be in a good mood. Alice was the kind of girl who's always in a good mood. A nice girl, all in all. Okay. We stopped in front of Marco's. Back to square one. We shook hands.

"I need to talk to you tomorrow."

"I'll call you," I answered. Then I added: "Be careful not to make too much noise going in. Because of your grandmother." I was just kidding, but you could tell by his face that the shot hit home, because Marco was always trying to make people believe that he lived alone, like a college student. He never told the truth, anyway, never. Then Alice stepped out of the taxi, and I wondered what was going to happen. But they just kissed goodnight on the sidewalk, sort of coolly and all, and she came and sat back down next to me. I thought that was strange. We watched Marco open the door and disappear. It hadn't been his night. But that couldn't be helped. We all have days when we're up, and days when we're not. Alice gave me a little smile. In spite of a bad beginning, this was more of an up day for me. Even though night had fallen long ago.

Chapter 13

Then I had to answer the driver's question, which was: "Where do you want to go next?" He could have been talking to Alice or to the two of us. "Where are you going?" I asked her. She gave the driver her address, and for my benefit added, "It's at the foot of the Eiffel Tower." It helped that she'd answered the driver so promptly. Because I didn't know where I was going, as it happened. If he'd asked where to drop me off, I probably would've answered the same thing: "At the Eiffel Tower." It would've been sort of dumb, since that neighborhood's pretty dead, especially in the middle of the night. But I doubt I would've had any better ideas. To tell you the truth, I don't know Paris all that well, even though I've lived here my whole life. Nine times out of ten, most people who live in Paris don't know it well, either. No kidding. If you asked them where they wanted to be dropped off and they hadn't thought about it, nine times out of ten they'd say: "At the Eiffel Tower," like by reflex. I think it's crazy.

What was also crazy was that to get there, we drove right down my street. It gave me a weird feeling. I almost told Alice, but she wouldn't have understood why I didn't get out, since we were at my place. I tried to see through the window if the lights in the living room were on. But I couldn't see very well: the taxi was driving too fast. Besides, I was discreetly checking out Alice's breasts, whose nipples were still erect. I wondered how the two of them managed it, never getting tired. Whatever. But at one point, I got the feeling she'd noticed me looking. In any case, she said:

"So tell me, this stuff about you and your teacher, is it true?"

I didn't know what to answer. So I decided to split the difference.

"Yeah, why? It's complicated, though. She's really in love. But for me, it's more like a casual girlfriend, see."

"But how old is she?"

"About thirty."

I couldn't believe it. Even I was impressed. I would've given anything for it to be true.

"It must be strange," she said, looking thoughtful.

"You know, age difference doesn't mean much these days. Look at Emilie Fermat's father's girlfriend. She's twenty."

"No way!"

"I swear."

But while we were chatting, I kept coming back to Alice's breasts. It was crazy: they were like magnets. Even if I tried to look her in the eyes, or look out the window, I automatically came back to them. At times, I had the impression they were talking to me, or signaling: "Hey, Julien! Hey there! Here we are!" It was driving me crazy. At that moment, I wanted to marry them. And settle down. Have a house, and all. And a car with lots of little breasts in the back seat. In other words, I was losing my mind.

It made me think of that comic book, I can't remember the title, but it was in the window of my neighborhood bookstore not long ago. The cover showed a girl opening her shirt, like an offering. You could see her breasts. Right on the cover. It was one of the most beautiful things I've seen in my life. Naturally, I went into the bookstore and started leafing through the comic book. I found the passage in the story where she shows her breasts. Two lovers are running through a forest because they're being chased by somebody or other. They manage to hide in some bushes somewhere. That's when the guy says to her, "Show them to me one last time." And the girl slowly unbuttons her shirt and opens it, while closing her eyes. So he could see. It was really beautiful, I swear. A woman who does that. For no reason, just out of generosity. On my way home from class, I used to make a little detour to pass by the bookstore window, like I had an important appointment. What cracked me up was that each time, there were a couple of little old guys on the sidewalk, pretending to look at the novels in the window. Perverts, for sure.

Once or twice, I considered kissing Alice. But we were already getting close to the Eiffel Tower area. And mainly, my mind was on Mathilde. I thought back to that moment I'd shared with her in her bedroom. And the thing about the study that was lit up all night long. So I turned to Alice to ask her opinion about it.

"Imagine a study, on the sixth floor of a building, say."

"Okay."

"All right. Now imagine that every night, the lights in the study are on. You know, like there was someone working instead of sleeping."

"Okay."

"All right. But imagine also that there's never anybody in that study."

"Okay."

"Nobody, you understand. It's always empty. Every night."

"So what?"

"What d'you think it means? Why is that study lit up every night if nobody works there?"

She thought about it briefly. Then, as the taxi pulled over to let her out, she said, "You have any more questions like that one?"

She didn't understand the poetry of the thing. But it must've been obvious that I was expecting a real answer, so she added: "I have no idea. Maybe the guy who works there always forgets to turn out the light when he leaves." That wasn't dumb. Even though I didn't think it was that. Then we exchanged a quick kiss good-bye and said so long. But while I was kissing her, I put my hand on her left breast, over her heart. I swear, I don't know what came over me. She stopped dead, but she didn't pull back. On the contrary. So I caressed it some more, like a lunatic who had three minutes to grab all the world's beauty. Then I said: "You going in?" She just said yes. As if it was obvious. Smiling the whole time. She opened the taxi door. The thing is, I should've gotten out with her. Even if she didn't let me go upstairs with her. Just to try. But I didn't dare. And I watched as she disappeared through the door of her building.

"What do we do now?" I asked the driver.

"Hey, I have no idea. You have to tell me."

"Let's go to the Gare Montparnesse," I answered, without knowing why there instead of somewhere else.

I was so turned on because of Alice's breasts, I nearly told the driver I wanted to go back to Porte Dauphine after all. Where I'd seen the women earlier in the evening. As a way of freeing myself from this obsession. But in the end, the station was a good idea. Because trains start running very early in the morning. In less than two hours, life will pick up again, I told myself. Two hours' wait won't kill me; I've had worse. Especially since most of the cafés around a train station probably open at dawn. I checked the time on the taxi dashboard: it was just past four in the morning. I watched as the deserted sidewalks streamed by the window. On the radio, they were playing "Que reste-t-il de nos amours?" It felt good. First thing tomorrow, I figured I'd call Madame Thomas to tell her that it was all over between us. I'd met another woman. Her name was Mathilde, and I wanted to marry her. In other words, I was out of my mind. And the music played on, melancholy and all. It felt good. I could've spent a couple of hours in that taxi, just driving around the city. Half asleep because of the liquor. Or else I could've asked the driver how much it would cost me to drive to the sea. Normandy is about two hours away, for example. I would get there almost at sunrise. That would be good, too. I'd let myself be rocked by the music during the entire trip. I had enough money for it. Then I'd walk along the beach. Before eating an enormous breakfast at a fancy hotel. And I'd send a message to Alice's breasts to tell them to come quick join me in the room I'd reserved with a view of the sea. But I didn't dare ask the driver that. The guy would have looked at me funny. Especially since it wouldn't be hard to figure out that I was running away from home. And you couldn't predict what his reaction to that would be.

I closed my eyes a little so I could imagine the sea. Which shows I was beginning to feel the fatigue. Actually, the seashore I like best isn't in Normandy, but Brittany. With the seagulls and all. Because my father took me there every summer in the old days. I don't remember what we did there very well anymore. I have images, of course, but they're a little blurry now, like everything having to do with my father. What I'd really like sometime would be to recall precise memories of everything I've already lived through. Even at my age, it would amount to a lot of stuff. I'm sure it would almost be enough to make me happy. I'd do what grandmothers do, spend half the day with their memories. What I understood from being with Madame Morozvitch is that grandmothers are happy most of the time. Inside their eyelids, they have images nobody else can see. Like treasures. They travel there, in their memory, away from the world. They resurrect people who have been dead for ages. They live with them, in fact. And from my point of view, you don't need to be a grandmother to live with the dead. For example, one thing I remember is that to go to Brittany with my father, we always left from Gare Montparnesse, and that before we took the train we always stopped at the Maison de la Presse, where he'd buy thousands of magazines, including a *Scrooge McDuck* comic book for me. The driver dropped me off next to the train station. It felt funny to realize that I'd once been at that exact spot with my father, even if it was a pretty lame thought. Places almost never change, in the end. We move around. But when you think of it, the world almost never moves.

I took out a fifty-euro note. The driver's eyes widened. He didn't have change, supposedly. I shrugged, to let him know he could keep it. I didn't give a damn. The guy couldn't believe it. I got the feeling he wanted to tell me something, but in the end he didn't say anything. Just started up and drove off. The night was so quiet, you could hear his engine for at least a minute. As if we'd been out in the country, in fact. Except that we were in the heart of Paris.

I walked around the station plaza for a while. It felt strange. You'd have thought it was the day after some huge catastrophe, where most Parisians had been wiped out. I imagined I was the last person alive. Because I'd thought to have a nuclear bomb shelter built under my bed. I really wonder what the heck I would do. In my opinion I would be really depressed after a few days. I would start to miss people—except for my mother, of course. Whatever. I went and sat down on a bench and lit myself a cigarette. I felt good. I gazed up at the Tour

Montparnasse, which looked immense from below. But after three minutes, I thought it wasn't a good idea to stay there. I couldn't sit still. So I decided to check out the neighborhood, to kill time. It was stupid to run away from home just to spend your time sitting on a bench doing nothing. There must be stuff happening in the neighborhood. At night, lots of things are going on everywhere, but secretly. You just have to look a little, and open the right doors.

My idea was to walk streets at random. And that's how I wound up on rue de la Gaîté, not too far from the station, after twenty minutes of wandering. I think it's a great name. I love it. I'd really like to live at this address: Julien Parme, 1, rue de la Gaîté. A little apartment that I would share with Mathilde, and a room on the top floor where I would write. No one would be allowed into that room. There would just be a table, a lamp, and thousands of books. That would be where I would write my greatest novels, for example. And my poetry. Just before they died, important people in the world of art would travel to rue de la Gaîté so they could meet me. And the ones who were in such lousy shape that they couldn't make the trip, their last wish on their deathbeds would be to say, "Read me a few more lines of Parme."

It was at that point in my daydreaming that I realized that rue de la Gaîté was actually crawling with porno bars. I swear. And also that I'd wound up in that street completely by accident. I think I really do have a knack, sometimes. At first, I couldn't quite figure out exactly what kinds of bars they were.

But they were the only things that looked alive in the whole neighborhood. Everything else was zonked out on sleeping pills. So I walked toward the lights, the only ones still on at that hour. That's how I discovered that all those sleazy places were closed, too. They just left the lights on all night long. Don't ask me why. But it let me take a good look. As if I were at the museum of sex, except you couldn't see much. A few photos of naked girls, but with black tape over the good parts. Too bad. I really wondered what happened inside, if there were also girls who stripped and showed their breasts, and especially whether you could do stuff with them, or if it was just for looking. It occurred to me that I could head over to Pigalle, where there had to be some of those places open. I don't know what it is with me and girls' breasts, but they blow me away. For girls' breasts, I'm ready to cross all of Paris. But then I started thinking about Mathilde again, and that worked better than a cold shower. It occurred to me that for all I knew, she was hoping that we would kiss, earlier. Maybe I had disappointed her. How could I know? Anyway, I don't understand anything about girls. Sometimes I understand, but it's always too late. It's like I'm blind. Even if sometimes I try to pretend I can see in the dark.

What the neighborhood also had were a million crêpe restaurants. They must be for Bretons, I decided. Before they catch their trains. Bretons eat crêpes. That's the way it is. Don't ask me why about that, either. At one point, I saw a shapeless mass on the ground—a bum. It made me uncomfortable to walk right by him. I would have liked to cross the street. But I didn't have time. As I passed him, I took a good look. He was asleep, wrapped in a really scuzzy sleeping bag. It made me feel bad. Until it occurred to me that I was sort of in the same situation. Seriously. For all I knew, he'd started out just like me: walking at night without knowing where to go. Telling myself that gave me a chill. I swear. Especially since right afterward, his dog, which I hadn't seen at first, pricked up his ears, stood up, and started following me. At first, it made me nervous. Some dogs are really aggressive. I know a guy who got bitten really bad by a dog like that. So I walked a little faster, but he started walking faster too. I didn't know what to do. So I stopped, and he stopped, too. He was doing every-thing I did, in other words. "Go back to your owner!" I whis-pered to him. "Go on! Git! Leave me alone." But he just stood there, looking at me. Actually, it wasn't hard to tell that this was a nice dog. At least he didn't at all look like a dog that would bite your arm off. "Go on, get out of here." But it was no use. He wouldn't listen. So I decided to act as if he wasn't there, and went on my way. At the end of the street, just before the boulevard, I turned around. He was still behind me, still giving me his "Take me with you" look. I didn't know what to do. It made me feel bad for the bum. He already didn't have much going for him. If he woke up and discovered that even his dog had abandoned him . . . Maybe it's just because he's hungry and his owner doesn't have anything to feed him, I thought. The stomach is always the real tyrant. I've heard it said that when bums have dogs, they spend all the money they get from begging on them. I swear. In fact most of the time bums are the least selfish guys you could imagine. Generous, even. Tender hearted.

Then the dog went ahead of me and crossed boulevard Montparnasse without even looking. Luckily, there were hardly any cars. It was practically deserted there, too. But it was still dangerous. I don't quite know what he was looking for. In any case, he was sniffing at stuff every ten yards. Having him flit around like that worried me, so I whistled to him, and he came back right away. A smart dog. At getting whatever he wanted. After that, he skipped around my feet like we were on our honeymoon. I would really have wanted to give him something to eat, but at that hour I couldn't see what. So I continued on my way and took rue de Rennes. He did, too. It was getting colder and colder, and I was starting to feel seriously tired. Suddenly rue de Rennes seemed endless to me. Really endless. A street that never ended. Like a moving sidewalk. Or in a nightmare, where you walk and walk, but you never get any closer to your goal. At some point you realize that there isn't any goal. And that hits you, of course. So you stop trying, you let yourself fall, and the moving sidewalk carries you right back to where you started. Life is often like that.

I can't tell you how long I walked that way. But when I turned around, the dog had disappeared. He must've gone back to his owner. So much the better, I thought. Still, I was surprised to see how dead the neighborhood was. I'd had the impression that incredible things happened at night, while everybody was sleeping. But strangely enough, the only impression I had there on the street was that in fact, everybody was sleeping. At the same time, I thought it must've been because I wasn't in the right place. What I had to do was to keep walking until I found something. I couldn't even say exactly what I was looking for. I walked along the quais by the Saint-Michel neighborhood. It was so depressing, you could die. Except that at one point I saw a bar that was open. It wasn't actually a bar, but a tavern. I swear, it was written on the facade. I thought that there were only taverns in Switzerland, and in the last century. But no, there was one right there by the Seine. That cracked me up. I peered through the window to see what it looked like. But you couldn't see anything. In any case, you can't see what most places look like from the outside. That way, customers have to come in. Clever. I really wasn't sure about opening the door. I wanted to. But at the same time, I wondered how people in the place would look at me. The problem is my size. I'd like to be really tall and everything. Because you can go anywhere when you're tall. People have trouble figuring exactly how old you are. I would've liked that. To be tall and well-built. It makes life easier, in my opinion. Whereas I have the unpleasant feeling of having my age slapped in my face at least thirty times a day. Especially in the way some people talk to you. They use a special tone of voice, as if you still sucked your thumb. That sort of thing just kills me. When I'm old, I'll talk normally to guys who are fourteen, fifteen years old. Like they were grownups. All of which is to say that I opened the door.

Chapter 14

I was surprised to see that the place was almost empty. Another bummer. I really wasn't having any luck. I should've gone to a nightclub after all. When people go out, that's where they must go. Not to taverns, anyway. I walked over and sat at the bar next to a guy with yellow hair. I don't mean blond, I mean yellow. Gray hair that had faded. He was the kind of guy who washed his hair along with his old underpants, if you see what I mean. His eyes were completely translucent. I swear. If I'd been a girl, I'm sure I would have thought he had super beautiful eyes. Sort of like a wolf's. He had an empty glass in front of him, and was counting his remaining coins to see if he had enough for another round. A drunk, I thought to myself. But with his hair, he looked pretty amazing. He could've been an actor, if he'd wanted to. I lit a cigarette, and continued to look at him, fascinated. He was really amazing.

Eventually, he noticed me. That's one of my magic powers. When I want someone to turn around, I start to look at them, like really intensely, and I don't stop. I concentrate, I concentrate, I send invisible waves, and at some point the guy always turns around, as if he could feel my invisible waves tickling him. I swear. It's one of my magic powers, which I learned from an old gypsy woman. Just kidding. Anyway, he wound up noticing me. He picked up his empty glass, as if we were toasting each other, and gave me a little nod. A way of saying hello, in other words. I'd really like to have known what kind of life a guy like that had led, with that hair. And especially why he had eyes like that. They were so translucent, you got the impression they could've started crying for no reason, just poetically.

After a while I offered him my pack of cigarettes, but he refused. Then I signaled to the bartender, who hadn't realized I was there and looked kind of startled when he saw me. I asked the yellow guy what he was drinking, and said it was on me. He couldn't believe that someone as young as me was buying him a drink. He and the bartender looked at each other, wondering if I was joking, but he finally said, "In that case, I'll have another one." The bartender turned to me and I said, "The same," without knowing what I was ordering. But I didn't care. I didn't plan to touch my drink. I'd already drunk too much, even though the walk had sobered me up a lot.

After that, the yellow guy and I didn't quite know what to say to each other. It wasn't easy to start a conversation. The bartender brought the two glasses. I was really surprised that he didn't ask my age or anything. He must have thought I was over sixteen, which made me happy. You could tell right away this bartender had class. As I watched, the yellow guy started to drink.

He knew what he was doing. When he put down his glass, he saw that I was looking at him. That must have bothered him because we hadn't said anything yet, and I hadn't touched my drink, so he said, "Looks like things aren't going so well for you." I put on an unhappy expression. I was just fooling around. If he'd said I looked happy, I would have started to smile. "Not so hot," I answered. And at that, I felt like I wanted to die. He just sighed and said, "Ah, that's life . . ." the way you do when you don't really feel like talking. Then after a pause, he continued.

"What's happening?"

"Nothing but troubles," I said.

But I could tell he wasn't that interested. So when the bartender came by again, I signaled that I wanted to pay. As they watched, I pulled out my wad of bills. That gave them a jolt. They looked at each other, as if trying to figure where I'd gotten all that money. I put the wad back in my pocket, pretending not to notice that I had impressed the hell out of them. When the bartender walked away, the yellow guy picked up the conversation. Now I intrigued him. Awful, how money can change any soul at all.

"So what problems are you having?" At that, I started to tell him everything. Up to then I hadn't been able to tell anyone what had been happening to me. And when important things happen to you, you want to share them. It's natural. Even with someone you don't know. So that's what I did. I started by telling him that I'd run away from home. So he'd understand, I said right away that it wasn't because of my father, since he was dead. It was because of the man who was trying to take his place. And because of my mother, of course.

My saying right off the bat that my father was dead stopped the conversation cold. But what made me feel bad was that as I said it, I felt like I was talking about something totally banal, whereas up to then I'd always had the opposite feeling, that what happened to me was amazing. Sort of like the yellow guy's head.

"How did your father die?"

I don't know what came over me then. Instead of telling him the truth, I shaded things. Just a little, but still. So he wouldn't be bored, I suppose.

"Officially, he was sick—his lungs. But the truth is, my mother killed him."

His translucent eyes widened, like in a horror movie, and he took a long swallow from his glass. Put yourself in his place. You're having a quiet drink at a bar, and some guy shows up and buys you another drink. Fine. Then he starts a conversation, and in the third sentence says that his mother killed his father. Scares the hell out of you, right? The yellow guy put down his glass and looked at me with his translucent eyes. I was almost afraid he could read my mind. Some people can do that. I swear. Anyway, he looked me in the eye, and finally asked the question I was waiting for, namely, how did my mother do it? I told him that the guy she moved in with afterward was a doctor, and that he was the one who stated that the cause of death was the lung disease, whereas actually it was clear that my mother had poisoned him. I'd found the pills she used and all. Some sort of rat poison. So the yellow guy would understand, I told him I was the one who found my father dead in the living room when I came back from school one day. His tongue was sticking out, like a dog that had been strangled. That's when I thought to say that in addition to the drugs, he'd also been strangled. My mother couldn't have done that, because she wasn't strong enough, so she'd had an accomplice. And I think the accomplice was the doctor she moved in with and who she wanted me to live with. As I said that, I was thinking about François, of course.

My guy looked completely blown away. Of all the things he'd heard in his life, this was probably the most off the wall. I could see he was thinking hard. About why my father had been strangled after being poisoned, for example. In general, when you poison a guy, it's so you don't have to strangle him later. Unless the pills don't work fast enough and you're afraid he'll have time to call the police or something. That's probably what my yellow guy was thinking. In any case, he looked shocked by my story. And also by the fact that his glass was already empty. So I gestured to the bartender, who right away poured him another drink, since it was on me. I hadn't touched my own drink yet. "I'm trying to quit," I told the bartender. Then I continued making up stuff about my life. It did me a world of good to be able to confide in someone. "So after that, what do you suppose I did?" He shrugged. He didn't know what I'd done after that. Neither did I, for that matter. "I couldn't live with them, knowing what I knew. And you can imagine how much I hated my mother." He nodded, or else he was scratching his nose, I couldn't tell. "Honestly, she was the worst mother in the world. Just the idea of sharing an apartment with her was too much. It really killed me. I wanted her dead. Things between us were very tense, because she knew that I knew. We fought all the time. She was always yelling at me. And I felt that my father was looking at me through the walls and accusing me of betraying him, if you see what I mean. I couldn't forget my father. He was always there, behind me—or above me, it depended. I was afraid he would say that it didn't seem to bother me to go on living with the woman who had killed him. I was afraid he would see me as an accomplice, you know? It was horrible. So what could I do?" Again, he didn't know, but I didn't give him time to say so. I went right on: "I started to run away. I ran away so many times they decided to stick me in a boarding school. That way at least they wouldn't have to worry. But it wasn't an ordinary boarding school. It was called Les Roches Noires. Ever hear of it?"

"Sounds familiar," he answered, but I could tell it was just so I wouldn't think he was ignorant. Or else because he didn't want to contradict me, given the life I'd led.

"It was a horrible place. Les Roches Noires is where they send the biggest assholes on Earth when people can't deal with them anymore."

He didn't seem to really know much about the place, so I told him a few things I'd experienced there, which my friend

Ben had told me about, plus a few details I'd picked up. For example, I said that the main problem with Roches Noires was that the kids in the school—from the twelve-year-olds to the fifteen-year-olds—were all housed in the same building. And the older boys often went to the floor where the twelve-year-olds slept, to have some fun. Sometimes they beat them up, and if you told, the next time was worse. So nobody said anything. But the dormitory toilets were an absolute horror. If you got up at night to go piss and you ran into them, they forced you to do things that were so disgusting, you wanted to die. I was twelve when I got there, and they did dirty things to me for a long time. Every Sunday night, before I had to return to the school, I was so frightened I would be shaking. This went on for two years. I almost jumped out a window several times, I was so scared when I heard them coming into the dorm. Especially because the floor monitor never said anything. I couldn't understand why. In a word, it was really violent. And the most violent of them all was the gang leader, Yann Chevillard. A real asshole, who made my life miserable for more than two years. He was always punching kids, humiliating them in front of everybody, and forcing them to do filthy things in the dorm toilets.

My yellow guy couldn't believe his ears. As I was telling him all this, I realized that it was true—I hadn't had an easy life. And it sort of moved me. It had been hard, but I'd finally pulled through. He was looking at me funny. I was sort of his hero. I paused to come up with more ideas, but also to have a drink. Laying out my whole life for him like this had made me thirsty.

But it was also a way to stop telling lies. Because I could've continued this way indefinitely, and after all, I had to stop at some point. I started working on my drink, but he said, "What happened then?" so I continued. It was his fault.

"After that, I ran away from the boarding school. I couldn't stand it anymore. I was so miserable. But my mother wouldn't have any of it. She refused to believe that I wasn't happy there. She wanted as few problems as possible, and to see me as little as possible. She didn't want me on her hands, in other words, especially since she and her new boyfriend were trying to have another kid."

"Oh yeah?"

"Yeah. And they had one, too, the next year. They gave him the same name as me. As if I didn't exist."

"That's not very nice. And what is that name?"

"Jean," I answered, because of Jean de la Fontaine.

We shook hands, but briefly, because I wanted to go on with the story of my life. I was on a roll and I couldn't stop. It felt incredibly good to confide in someone. "So I ran away from the boarding school. It happened the night Yann Chevillard's gang caught me in the toilets. They stripped me naked. They held my arms and legs. I was at their mercy. And one of the guys had a knife, I swear. A box cutter, actually. He pretended he was going to cut off my prick. But the worst is, he could have done it, they were such psychos. He brought the blade closer, and I screamed, but one of the others put his hand over my mouth so no one could hear me. I really thought that douchebag was going to cut it off. Then the one who had his hand over my mouth to keep me from screaming for help took it away, and Yann Chevillard, who was standing over me, started pissing on my face, so I had to close my mouth and couldn't scream. And one of the guys, the one with the box cutter, told me to open my mouth or he'd cut my prick off. I had to make like a urinal, and swallow it all, afterward. It was a nightmare. So I decided to leave that very night. How?" I paused, to build suspense. And also to get him involved. But he didn't react. "By sneaking out, plain and simple. It was snowing. I walked to the train station, and I took the first train for Paris. I didn't have any money. I spent the whole trip hiding in the bathroom. I was scared the conductor would bust me and report me to the police. Then in Paris I found some acquaintances who were kind enough to hide me and help me start over again. Everyone was looking for me. My photo was posted in the train stations. I was in a tough spot. If you want to know how I pulled through, you can read the biography written about me. You'll see that I was lucky enough to meet a wonderful woman who hid me in her room. She was a lot older than me. She must've been around thirty. She worked as a French teacher. She gave me back my will to live. Anyway, that's how it happened."

The yellow guy was totally blown away. His glass was empty, and the bartender served him another drink without even asking. Then he set another one down next to mine, which I hadn't finished yet. Like my story. So I continued: "Still, I had to do something to keep busy, so I started to write. When I tell them that, journalists all over the world always think it's out of modesty. They can't believe that boredom can be the source of genius. They always think there must be a better reason. But for me, that was exactly it—boredom. And also to unburden myself of the secret that only I knew. Namely, that my mother had killed my father . . . and that he was buried in our own garden!"

I was seriously out of control now. But the yellow guy didn't even notice. He was swallowing everything I told him. To clinch it, I added: "Under the apple tree!" But he didn't react. Though he didn't look stupid.

Just then the bartender came over. He put both hands on the counter, as if to say that this was his place, and asked me:

"So, are you a student?"

His breaking my momentum annoyed me, especially to ask such a lame question.

"Not really," I answered. "I'm a writer." And I lowered my eyes, out of literary modesty.

"A writer? Really? How old are you?"

The bartender frowned, as if I couldn't possibly be a writer. At the same time he was flattered that I'd come to his tavern, in spite of my notoriety and my international career. Luckily a guy at the other end of the bar called to him just then, and he went over. I turned to the yellow guy, who was finishing his drink with difficulty. He was probably waiting for the end of my story. But I didn't want to come across like someone who does nothing but complain and all. Because I'd had quite a bit of luck, afterward. My books were published and they sold very well, I said. Better than very well, even. It's quite rare for someone to be successful so young. I'd traveled to a fair number of countries for my translations. People pretty much everywhere consider me one of the best writers of my generation.

"So everything's fine," the yellow guy concluded.

It's true, I was getting a little mixed up, with my stories about being successful. After all, I'd started out telling him that things weren't going at all well. I was attached to the story of my success, but now I had to find something killer to explain the collapse.

"Everything *was* fine," I corrected him. "Everything was fine until I screwed it all up."

I took a long drink from my glass—it was beer—while wondering just exactly what I'd done to screw it all up. But the yellow guy wasn't asking for details; he was almost asleep. I continued: "Because my obsession was to find Yann Chevillard, the shit who led the gang of fifteen-year-olds. After all those years. And it just so happened Chevillard was living in Paris. He was twenty now. It wasn't hard to track down his address—that's what phone books are for! So I had his address. He lived near Gare Montparnasse, on rue de la Gaîté, to be exact. When I found out he lived there, I knew right away I was going to do something really stupid. I began hanging around his neighborhood, and one evening I ran into him. I recognized him right away. It was Yann Chevillard all right. I followed him, and when he opened the door to his building, I walked in with him. He didn't recognize me, which proves that he wasn't very well read. Anyway, he climbed the stairs, and I followed him up. I was a little nervous. Because I knew I was going to do something reckless. In fact look, my hands are still shaking. Oh yeah, I forgot to tell you that it happened a little while ago . . . Just before I came here."

I held out my hands and shook them so that he would understand how the event had affected me.

"So I was behind him in the stairwell, following him. I let him get one floor ahead of me. Earlier that day, I'd taken a knife I found in Madame Thomas's kitchen, the woman I was living with. I could feel the knife's terrible weight in my pocket. To steel myself, I thought back on all the horrors Chevillard had inflicted on me, and probably on other kids my age. I was going to make him pay for everything he'd done. A stab in the back, that would be the final reckoning. I waited until he was in front of his door. He'd put his key in the lock. I stepped right behind him. Just a few feet away. I could strike whenever I wanted to. He was at my mercy. He turned around, surprised to see me there . . ."

Just then, the bartender came over to us and interrupted me, right when I was deep into my story, with Yann Chevillard on the building landing and the knife in my right hand.

"So no kidding, you're really a writer?"

I grimaced.

"Leave him alone," said my yellow friend, who seemed to be waking from a long nap. "Can't you see he's got a broken heart?"

A broken heart. That killed me.

"Oh, I'm sorry."

"No, no," I said, looking heartbroken. "In any case, that's life . . . You have to learn to live with it."

There was a brief silence. The bartender must've understood that this wasn't just any heartbreak, given the way I looked. And it's true, I started to feel heartbroken. My life suddenly seemed like a stupid enterprise, a useless prison, an empty promise. I felt like dying.

"Do you know the difference between playing tennis and making love?" he asked, probably to cheer me up.

"What?" I didn't see the connection.

"Do you know the difference between playing tennis and making love?"

"No."

"Then keep on playing tennis!" he said. He nearly choked with laughter, and so did the yellow guy.

I couldn't believe it. Compared to my heartbreak, there was something fatuous about their laughter that I found inappropriate. Inappropriate and embarrassing. How could they be laughing their heads off like that when I was teetering at the edge of the abyss? In any case, nobody takes me seriously in this country. I decided to leave that place, where people make fun of your heartbreak. I put down the money and left, feeling irritated and suicidal.

I was fed up. I really wanted extraordinary things to happen to me, but nothing was happening. Daybreak wasn't far off.

In any case, it felt like the start of a new day. Not yet, really, but you could feel it would happen soon. I continued walking along the Seine. I went down to the quai. It was a good place to hang out. I was dying to get some sleep. I felt exhausted, so I stretched out on a bench near a weeping willow. I think I slept a little, but I kept waking up, so I was always between the two. There's nothing more pleasant, I find. At times, I could hear seagulls crying. I don't know if you're aware of it, but there are lots of seagulls along the banks of the Seine that come from Le Havre and follow the barges up to Paris. Then, when I was fully awake, I went to find a bistro for a cup of coffee. Because I didn't want people to see me. It was daylight, and I could be spotted, especially given my age. Luckily, there isn't a soul on the quais on Saturday mornings. I didn't have to look far for the coffee. I went into a place called La Frégate on the other side of the street, and ordered breakfast to get my energy back. It did me a world of good, but afterward, I wanted to sleep more than ever. There were already a few people around, even though it was super early. Because on Saturday, people don't go to work; most of them get up much later. As I was thinking that, I realized that here it was, Saturday, my first sleepless night, or almost. But the thing was, I had an incredible headache. It hurt so much I couldn't think. Because of what I had drunk. It was almost as awful as my first hangover. Though I must say I don't remember my first hangover: I'd been loaded.

I asked the waiter if there was a small hotel in the neighborhood. My reason was, I had just arrived in Paris. He told me about a place two minutes away. The Hôtel du Quai Voltaire, it was called. I walked there, my headache getting worse and worse. I'd asked the waiter if he had some aspirin he could give me, but he said he wasn't allowed to give aspirins to customers. I didn't quite understand why. Whatever. The Hôtel du Quai Voltaire didn't look like much, but I didn't give a damn. I swear, all that interested me was to hit the hay for a couple of hours. I walked up to the guy at the front desk. He looked me up and down. You can imagine how I looked. I asked if they had any rooms, but I didn't wait for him to answer. Right away, I took out my credit card. Well, François's. I felt that this threw him off balance. He checked his register or something. I could see what he was about to do. So I felt I had to tell him something. Like I had just come to Paris. To meet my future publisher. It was only for the weekend. After that I had to return to Bordeaux, because of school. He gave me a funny look. Then he said, "You've written a book?" I felt he was looking at me differently now. He was impressed to have Julien Parme in front of him. In the flesh. He said I looked young. I shrugged modestly.

Then he gave me a room number, explaining that it faced the quai but that the windows were double glazed. I said fine, and handed him the card. It occurred to me that for all I knew, François had told the bank to freeze it. I felt nervous as hell. I typed in the code. The guy was still looking at me oddly. But I pretended not to notice, so as not to make him even more suspicious. Luckily, the card worked. He looked relieved, and gave me the keys.

I went up to the third floor. The inside of the hotel really wasn't very nice looking. The hallway carpet looked like it belonged to some provincial grandmother who was about to croak, if you know what I mean. But I didn't care. I wasn't there for the decor. I opened the door to my room, which was real small. Right away I went into the bathroom to splash some water on my face. Then I stretched out on the bed, without even getting undressed or anything. And collapsed.

Part III

The Elephants

Chapter 15

When I woke up, I had no idea where I was. The feeling lasted a long time, but then it suddenly all came back to me. I hadn't bothered to close the curtains, and now stood blinking in the Saturday morning sunshine. It was almost pleasant, like being on vacation. The first thing I did was to go drink from the faucet in the bathroom—two liters of water, at least. Then I lit the last cigarette in my pack, which was also my first one of the day. I opened the window so I could smoke in the fresh air. The noise from the quais rose up to me, but delayed, because of my headache. There were a heck of a lot of cars now. Traffic was jammed. You had a view of the Louvre and a bridge across the way. It was really terrific. I stood there looking at all that, getting my thoughts in order. What time could it be? Using the phone on the night table, I called the front desk. They told me it was almost 2 p.m. I couldn't believe it. Two in the afternoon already! I had really slept a lot. And right away I thought of my mother. I went back to the window so that the whole room wouldn't reek of cigarettes. My mother . . . By now, she was probably looking for me everywhere. The first thing she would've done would be to call Marco, to find out where I'd gone. I wanted to call Marco myself so he could tell me if there was any news. I went back to the night table and dialed his number, but he didn't answer. Nine times out of ten, Marco doesn't answer. It winds up getting on your nerves. I hoped he hadn't snitched on me to my mother, about my thing with Madame Thomas.

Then I took a shower to really wake myself up. It wasn't bad, standing under the shower like that, doing nothing. Unfortunately, they had forgotten to give me any soap. But hey, I'm not a complainer. I spent at least twenty minutes in the shower. I dried myself off, wrapped myself in a white towel, and stretched out on the bed. I was having trouble getting going. The room had a little table with stationery and envelopes. I liked that. Writers are always happy to see a little table with stationery and envelopes. There was no TV, on the other hand. Too bad. I thought of writing a letter to my mother. To explain things to her, and to say good-bye. That was an idea. Then she'd stop looking for me. She'd understand that I wanted to live my life without her. I closed my eyes, and thought that my mother must be worried as hell. After all, it must really freak you out to come in one morning and see that your son isn't there. I tried to imagine what I would do in her place. She would think to check with my friends, of course, and also at Emilie Fermat's. She must suspect that I'd snuck out to go to the party. That bothered me a little. I didn't want Mathilde to find out about it that way.

She wouldn't understand. And she'd think I hadn't been straight with her the night before, especially if the story about Madame Thomas ever got back to her. To tell you the truth, that was what I was mainly nervous about. Maybe I should warn her myself, I thought. Besides, that would be an excuse to see her. Because I really had better come up with an excuse if I ever wanted to see her again.

I spent a pleasant moment turning this idea over in my mind. I'm never too swift in the morning. Anyway, I didn't have Mathilde's phone number—not her cell, not her landline, nothing. Marco probably had the landline, so I tried to reach him again, but he didn't pick up. Shit. Then I suddenly remembered that she went riding in the Bois de Boulogne on Saturdays. Maybe I could go there and see her. And talk with her. And kiss her, finally. Or else write her a letter to ask her to meet me in the bar of the Hôtel du Quai Voltaire. That was a possibility, too. And above all, it was cool.

I went to sit at the little table. There was a menu with stuff to eat you could order that they would deliver right to your room. I looked it over. There were just sandwiches. But I wasn't at all hungry, in any case. I couldn't have eaten a thing. My throat felt like sandpaper. I took out the stationery—letterhead paper, no less. That way, Mathilde would know where to reach me: 19, quai Voltaire. My letter would explain that I'd had to leave home and was going to Italy soon, but that I absolutely had to see her first. That was perfect. And I started searching for the right words to tell her. But it wasn't easy to explain everything in just a few lines. Even for a writer. I stood up and dialed Marco's number again, but in vain. So I went back to sit in front of my blank page. I was even more blocked than usual. Finally, I got started: "Dear Mathilde . . ." No, that sounded like a letter you'd write to a cousin. It should just be "Mathilde." I tore up the page and took another one, also with a letterhead. "Mathilde . . ." In search of inspiration, I went to the window and looked over at the Louvre. What should the next words be? To think that at one time the Louvre was the king's personal hangout . . . Those old-time kings, they didn't screw around. Living the good life. I'm a royalist, anyway. I remember that when I was a kid, what I wanted more than anything was to be a prince. I don't know why. You drag some things around in your head without quite knowing why. Most of the time they're pretty lame.

I went back to sit down at my table. Maximum concentration. "Mathilde . . ." When you came right down to it, maybe writing her a letter wasn't such a good idea. The age of letters is over. We still have the time to write them, but we don't have the time to wait for them, so nobody writes anymore. "Mathilde, I would like you to know . . ." No. That sounded official. The best would be something short but precise, to make it clear that she absolutely had to meet me at the hotel. Otherwise I would be leaving for Italy without seeing her again. I started daydreaming about Italy. Venice and all. Then I went back to the job at hand. I tore up the sheet and took another one. I recopied my opening: "Mathilde . . ." I reread it several times. So far, it was fine. I had the right tone. Letters are all a matter of tone. "Mathilde, I have to talk with you." I paused to reread it. "Mathilde, I have to talk with you." I really do have literary talent, don't I? "Mathilde, I have to talk with you. For very complicated reasons, I had to leave home. I'm not going back." Oh boy! . . . I stood up, frankly fascinated by the power of those three sentences. Standing at the window I repeated "I'm not going back" three times to myself, then aloud I added "ever again." I ran to my table to quickly write down my "ever again" before I forgot it. It's always the same with good ideas: if you don't pin them down right away, they evaporate and are forgotten. "For very complicated reasons, I had to leave home. I'm not going back ever again." Not bad at all. But I had a terrible moment of doubt. What if somebody came across this letter, with the letterhead? They would be able to find my hiding place. Maybe it wasn't smart to leave any written clues around. Though to be honest, what I was especially afraid of was what Mathilde would think of my letter.

That reminded me of what happened once with my witch of a stepsister Bénédicte when I let her read a short story I'd written. I have to tell you the whole story, so you'll understand my problem. It had happened about three months before. I had written a short story. Fifteen pages without any mistakes. Practically a novel, in other words. I had read it over about thirty times before coming to the objective conclusion that it was a little gem. The story was about a guy who wakes up one day and has lost his memory. Just like that. And when he finds out what his old life was like, he goes crazy. Pretty original, if you ask me. I called it "A Thousand Years of Solitude." Which shows that it was really very good. I was really proud of it. So I wanted Bénédicte's opinion on the subject. Her opinion wasn't all that important to me, it's just that I figured she might have something to say to me. Like pay me compliments.

Bénédicte wasn't super well read, of course. She'd never read La Fontaine, for example. But with my short story "A Thousand Years of Solitude" I was writing for the general public, too. At first, I even thought of calling it "A Hundred Thousand Years of Solitude." You get the idea. Anyway, I left it lying around the living room—accidentally on purpose, my standard technique—waiting for Bénédicte to find it. I was positive she would read it. It was just like her to read things that didn't belong to her. She'd even be capable of opening letters that weren't addressed to her.

It worked like a charm. That very evening, my short story disappeared. I could practically see her face already. She would suddenly realize that she'd been living with a genius of French literature for nearly two years and hadn't suspected a thing. Under the very same roof, too. I could already see her weeping in my arms, begging me to forgive her for being awful to me those last months. And I would say, "That's all right, I hate you not."

But there was no reaction from her. It became stranger and stranger. At one point we ran into each other in the kitchen. I'd been hanging around for at least an hour, waiting for her to come out of her room. She was calmly pouring herself a glass of milk when she said, almost absentmindedly: "By the way, I read your short story." I straightened myself to a dignified height, ready to receive the acclaim of the people. "And?" She finished her milk. Having to praise me must really cost her. She set her glass down on the table, pausing to find the right words. Because she now knew that I was extremely careful that words be the right ones. "It's really lousy," she finally said. "What?" "Your story is ridiculous. It's not believable, not for a second. Honestly, it's really boring."

I knew it! She hadn't understood a thing, as usual. It's crazy, how that girl was irremediably herself. Totally predictable. She hadn't even understood that the whole point of the story wasn't the plot at all, but the style. Just the style! Except that after that right away, she added, "And just between the two us, you can't write for shit." That demolished me. I rushed over to wring her neck, but she ran to her room bleating like a nanny goat. In any case, she couldn't possibly understand. Poetry was something she'd probably never heard of. And it was too demanding a text for a girl like her. But to tell you the truth, it did hurt me a little. As an artist, I mean. And I wouldn't want Mathilde to think the same thing, reading my letter: that you can try to flush my writing away, but it always floats to the top.

Suddenly I had the idea of the century. And the next one, too. I picked up the telephone again and called Information for the Bois de Boulogne riding club. I wanted to talk to Mathilde face to face. It was less risky than a letter. The Club du Jardin, it was called, apparently because it was in the Jardin d'acclimatation. The operator asked me if I wanted to be connected. I said yes. Then I got a girl with a kind of slurred voice, as if she'd just gotten up, and I asked her what time Mathilde Fermat had her class. I explained that I was her brother and that she'd forgotten to tell me when to pick her up. "Five p.m.," the girl said. I hung up, feeling proud of my trick.

Then I left my room. I had to do some shopping to get ready for what would happen next. First I decided to go back to rue de Rennes, where I'd seen tons of phone stores. I wanted to buy myself a cell phone. It would be more convenient. I walked down the two flights, hoping not to run across the desk clerk from the morning. Something about his looks didn't inspire a whole lot of confidence. So as not to be noticed, I walked by him without stopping. He just said, "Have a nice day, mademoiselle." That killed me. But it was actually a different desk clerk, and he hadn't had the time to see me properly because I was walking so fast. Otherwise he would never have said that to me.

It did me good to be outside walking around. But at the same time, I really felt as if I was on the run. Every time a car passed, I was afraid it would be my mother or someone, and I immediately turned my head away. It was a stupid reflex, I admit, considering that there really wasn't much chance of us running into each other by accident. Paris is a maze. But I couldn't help it, what can I say? It was all I thought about. So I kept walking, incognito like, to the top of rue de Rennes. And guess who I ran into there? Not my mother, luckily, but that girl whose name

I've forgotten and whom I'd seen the night before at Emilie Fermat's. Mount Everest, the super-tall blonde who had kindly let me finish her glass of champagne. She walked by me without stopping, even though our eyes met. I'm sure she didn't recognize me or anything. But it reminded me that you're never safe from bumping into just about anybody.

I went into a store. It was pretty crowded, since it was Saturday. All the salespeople wore identical red vests. Just because of that, I could never work in a store like that. Too totally lame. The girl in line ahead of me was totally clueless. She was asking the dumbest questions in the world. You almost thought she did it on purpose. They were almost at the level of, Which way do you hold the phone? I swear. A real moron. It had to be the first cell she'd ever bought. Really stupid, and fat, too. Honestly, you wonder how some people go on living. Then another salesman approached me. I told him what I needed, namely a cell with a prepaid card. Since I didn't have any ID or anything. It took me all of three minutes to make my choice, while the fat girl was asking why her cell phone didn't have a wire. I swear. I walked past her to go pay, smiling ironically. But I wasn't alone. I could sense that the other clerk, the one who was waiting on her, wanted to laugh, too. He couldn't, though, since his job was to help her buy a phone, after all. Whatever. I handed over my credit card and typed in the code, but the terminal made a strange noise. "It isn't going through," I was told. I pretended to be surprised. They tried again, but the same thing happened. So I paid cash. Damn. I was sure François had told his bank to freeze the card. That scared me.

Back out on the street, I called Marco right away. This time he picked up, which almost surprised me.

"Marco? It's Julien."

"Shit, what the hell have you been up to?"

He was quick on the uptake.

"How's it going?"

"Don't you know everybody's looking for you? I had no idea what happened. Where are you? Your mother told me you took off. Is that right? Damn, at least you could've let me know."

"Don't sweat it."

"She called me this morning, first thing. At dawn. She thought you were at my place."

"Hey, I'm not that dumb."

"Actually, you are that dumb. What got into you? Tell me, where are you, right now?"

"I'm not alone," I answered, to get his imagination working.

"You're at Madame Thomas's, is that it?"

"How do you know?"

"Deductive reasoning, buddy. But why'd you take off like that? Are you nuts? We've gotta get together. Come to my place. We can talk quietly."

"Too risky. We can meet in a café, if you like."

"When?"

"Let's say seven o'clock. I can't make it any earlier."

"You mean 7 p.m.?"

"Yeah."

"Not before then? All right, fine. Where?"

I didn't want to meet in a neighborhood that was too popular, so as not to run into anyone I knew. The best would be to have Marco come someplace not far from my hotel. I looked around.

"Listen, there's a place called Le Marché. On rue de Rennes. Is that okay for you?"

"Le Marché . . . All right. See you later."

"Okay, bye."

We hung up. Marco had sounded weird on the phone. I imagined that he was actually standing next to my parents, with the cops there, for all I knew, and they were all trying to make him spill the beans. The idea gave me a chill. And right away I decided that going to the meeting might be dangerous. Then I thought I'd try withdrawing money with François's credit card, to see if it was really frozen, or if the phone store's terminal was just on the blink. In that neighborhood there was practically nothing but cash machines. I stopped at the one at the post office. Don't ask me why that one rather than another. As I feared, I couldn't get any money. Shit. I really should have withdrawn some that morning, at dawn. Before my mother found out I was gone. I thought about it. Bénédicte usually didn't have any Saturday classes and it was my teacher training day, so nobody had any reason to get up especially early. And when I'd paid for my breakfast at La Frégate, the card had worked fine. It was stupid of me not to have thought about this sooner. But I figured it would take François longer to realize that I'd taken his credit card. It was as if the first thing he did when he woke up was to run to his card to see if it had slept well.

After that I went to a drugstore. I bought a thing with herbs to smell good, a toothbrush, and a box of aspirin. I left the store and walked toward my hotel. My idea was to charge my new cell phone, because it kept beeping to warn me that the battery was dead. On my way I stopped in a bookstore right on the boulevard. Sometimes when I have time to kill, I enjoy walking around bookstores. I don't know why, it relaxes me. I looked to see what was for sale. And to see if they didn't happen to have a book by me. But I didn't spend much time there. I had to take a piss like crazy. I'm sorry to be so blunt, but it's true: I absolutely had to get back to the hotel. The thing is, in most novels the characters never seem to go to the bathroom, as if it were embarrassing. I think that's dumb and not at all believable. Anyway, in the novel I'm going to write, it won't be as if the characters are pure spirits. No. They'll also be bodies. For example, something I find really funny is that all those classical characters in Racine and the rest, we've been seeing them on stage for centuries now without their ever taking a leak. By now, they must be hurting. Probably writhing in pain. That's why they declaim those speeches, from holding it in. Centuries of holding it in. Sooner or later, they can't help it, they have to let something out. A matter of pressure. So they declaim. And then people are surprised that they can't act and they don't sound the way people talk in real life. Anyway, I went out of the bookstore and cut left toward the Seine and my hotel.

Once I was there, I didn't take the time to go up to my room. I'd just barely made it. So I went straight to the restroom in the bar, which was on the ground floor. I felt a shiver rise up my spine. Total bliss. Then, since I was there, I asked the guy at the bar for something to drink. He asked me what I wanted, but sort of rudely, so I said apricot juice, to give him a hard time. I sat down in a leather armchair and started to leaf through the newspaper lying there. Naturally I had been careful to plug the phone charger into a nearby outlet. So I was able to turn the cell back on. It was almost past four o'clock. When I finished my juice, it would be time to go if I didn't want to miss Mathilde at the Jardin d'acclimatation. But what would I tell her? That she moved me, for example. That when I saw her, I felt both happy and sad, and also a little ashamed. As if I was someone who wasn't good enough for her, or that she was too good for me. I don't know. And that sometimes when I saw her, I even felt I should take a bath.

But would she even understand what I was talking about?

Chapter 16

On the way to my room, I passed the same guy at the front desk. He had a weasel face and was starting to go bald, the kind of guy who pays girls to sleep with him, if you know what I mean. I gave him an awkward smile and quickly headed for the stairs. I really didn't want to get into a conversation with him. It could have led to trouble. Once in my room, I put down my things. I wet my hair and combed it, put on some cologne, and brushed my teeth. There, I was ready. I went back downstairs. I could tell that the desk clerk, from watching me parade past him, was wondering if I was planning some sort of dirty trick. Leaving the hotel, I wasn't sure which way to go to find the nearest métro station. A taxi would be for later. I couldn't afford to throw my money around right and left now; I had to be careful. I took a wrong turn, of course, and wound up at the Rue du Bac station, which I don't think was the closest one. But no matter; I'm young, I can still walk.

I went as far as Concorde, where I had to change to line 1, which would take me to Neuilly. As I walked through the tunnels to make the transfer, I saw a completely unbelievable scene. Something I might not even have noticed some other time. I mean on an ordinary day. I don't know if you've noticed it, but our faculty of observation gets anesthetized in the course of daily life. We don't feel anything anymore. We just go from one place to another, our eyes vacant. But on the days when we feel vulnerable, our sensitivity is always stronger, our awareness as sharp as a knife, and we perceive much subtler things. That's what I think. Which is why it's good to suffer from time to time, in my opinion. It forces us to open our eyes. And conversely, I feel that the worst thing is to not be able to suffer anymore. Some people are like that. Just to look at them, you understand that they're incapable of suffering, of feeling pain, of plunging into distress. They're always floating on the surface of things, like a lonely buoy that never experiences the ocean depths, the fishes, the sharks. They live so completely by habit that they go through their identical days without ever showing any sensitivity at all. I just don't get people like that. Because under those conditions, I don't see the point of living.

Anyway, what I saw was a guy fall down. He was walking along normally, and then suddenly—whump!—he fell to the ground. I was right behind him. It felt weird to see somebody fall. At first, I thought he was dead, like of a heart attack. In fact, he'd just had a dizzy spell, but it looked serious. In any case, the moment he hit the ground, everybody turned toward him. An old lady even gave a little scream. And within seconds, a dozen people were gathered around the guy, checking to see if he was dead or what. The problem was, nobody's cell phone could get a signal, so a young guy said he would call for help. When you saw him run, you would've thought he was a sprinter. He took off like a shot. Okay. Up to then, everything was pretty ordinary. But what happened for me is that at that moment I thought back to another scene I'd once witnessed in the métro that had really affected me. Let me tell you about it. I was in the métro, and a very ugly old woman, a homeless person, was at the end of the car; she really stank and she was barefoot. Nobody wanted to sit next to her because of the smell. And when I say she stank, that's not a metaphor. She was so dirty, she reeked. Anyway, she had the end of the car all to herself. I was watching her from where I was, and wondering what must be going through her mind. She looked a little crazy, to tell you the truth. Suddenly the same thing happened: she had a dizzy spell. She started moaning and drooling. I swear. Like in a horror movie. And yet—and this is what I wanted to tell you—nobody moved. Nobody. They didn't so much as lift a finger. And it wasn't only because of the smell. Maybe people figured that it was normal, that she often did that, I mean moan and drool, and that anyway it was none of their business. Except that in fact it *was* their business, the business of being willing to see somebody who was crying out and saying, "Help. Help me." But everybody just turned a blind eye. Like it wasn't happening. I wanted to do something, but I honestly didn't know what. I looked around, and since everybody seemed to think it was normal, I let myself be convinced. She could've croaked, in my opinion, but I wasn't able to check, since unfortunately my stop was next and I had to get off.

Okay. The comparison I wanted to make was that in the tunnel, everybody rushed over to the guy within seconds. So here's what I wondered: Why in one case does everybody act as if the dizzy spell wasn't happening, and in the other as if it was the only thing that mattered? The answer is obvious and you can see where I'm going with this, but it deserves to be developed some more. It's because of shoes. Because the real difference between the guy in the tunnel and the old lady in the métro is that one of them was wearing nice shoes and all, while the other was barefoot. In my opinion, to understand somebody it's almost enough just to look at their shoes. That's my theory. Responding to the guy with nice shoes, a guy of the world if you like, is just responding to a dizzy spell. That's all. And it's no trouble for anybody. Not in the least. Whereas responding to the old lady's dizzy spell was much more. It was risking facing this reality: that there are people walking the streets without shoes. And walking without shoes is a symptom of a reality that is even more complicated, and awful. I don't know if you see what I mean. Reacting to the crazy woman's dizzy spell meant forcing yourself to look at her, to accept the idea that she existed, to remember her, her presence, her chaos, her loneliness. We don't see things that we don't want to see. That's my theory, too. I don't know if you've noticed, but you get the impression that most people in the métro are blind. They don't meet anybody else's eyes except their own. Because their eyes are turned inward, as if they were trying to look at themselves from the inside. They look like ghosts. I swear. They could walk in front of a dead person without even noticing. But if you tell them there are people dying on the other side of the world, they'll sign any petition you like and say how outrageous it is.

I find that outrageous.

I got off at the Sablons station. Coming out into the open, I noticed that the weather was really beautiful. The sky was all blue and the light was almost dazzling. I had to walk another ten minutes to the entrance of the Jardin d'acclimatation. It had been ages since I'd been there. I seem to recall that the last time happened to be with my father, but I don't remember very well. I do remember that I once went on the merry-go-round a few times but wasn't allowed to visit the shooting gallery, which really interested me. After a while, merry-go-rounds just go in circles, you know. Riding a horse already makes me sick, so if it isn't even a real horse, you may as well put a bullet in your head. A blank, of course.

You had to pay to get into the Jardin. That killed me. But hey, I wasn't about to quibble for a few pennies. I paid what I was asked, like a gentleman, and took the opportunity to ask where the riding club in question was. The girl who gave me directions had teeth that were spaced like a rodent's, and I didn't listen to her answer because I was so fascinated by someone who looked as if she never saw a dentist. It must not be easy for her. Of course, show me someone it's easy for, I'd like to meet them.

Seriously. Anyway, I didn't dare ask her again, because I didn't want to annoy her, so I walked straight ahead, figuring that I was sure to find the famous riding club eventually. I checked my cell: it was almost five o'clock. Mathilde would be coming in from her ride soon. I planned to wait for her, and then suggest she take a walk in the park with me. After that I could buy her some cotton candy if she wanted. And maybe hold her hand. Make a little headway, in other words.

There were lots of people in the park, I better tell you right away. Especially families. And kids everywhere—running, shouting, quarreling. In a way, it was like a gigantic nursery. A tiny little river ran along one side; a stream, really, and I followed it for at least ten minutes. What's cool in this park are the trees. They're all huge. I figure that when I came here with my father, those trees were already there, and for them it was like yesterday, that from their point of view nothing had really changed. At that, I felt that we were all minuscule. Like ants, except that we have worries in our head.

Suddenly my cell phone rang. That startled me, because I wasn't used to its ringtone. It could only be Marco. He was probably calling to change our appointment or say he would be late. Marco was physically unable to get anywhere on time. Even if he tried with all his might, he couldn't make an appointment on time. It was sort of a disease. Like his lying. I answered in the tone of voice of someone who already knows what kind of excuse you're going to come up with.

"Yeah?"

"Julien, it's me."

I practically had a heart attack, I swear. It was my mother's voice. I couldn't believe it. I hung up right away, and switched off the phone to keep her from calling me right back. I almost threw it on the ground, as if it were burning my hand. Damn. How did she get my number? The only possibility was Marco. I didn't see how she could have, otherwise. Which meant that son of a bitch had blabbed everything. I couldn't believe it. As if he'd set a trap for me. Oh boy, I thought. You think your friends are your friends, when in fact they're ready to sell you out at the drop of a hat. The thought destroyed me. The bastard! You can never trust anybody. This was Marco's revenge. The thing was, I had probably humiliated him the night before, with my story about Madame Thomas. For sure. I could imagine the scene. My mother goes to his place to talk to him, or maybe it's the cops, and Marco wets himself and tells them everything. The traitor. On the other hand, what made me laugh, though in an odd way, was imagining that he may have also told all about Madame Thomas. Like that I was secretly sleeping with her. Oh boy . . . This whole thing was getting weirder and weirder. I imagined the cops showing up at Madame Thomas's to see if I was there. The look on Madame Thomas's face, when they told her that everybody knew about our love affair. No kidding, I started laughing out loud, but it was probably just nerves. In any case, I could forget about my meeting with Marco. Because that was less a meeting than a trap.

I finally reached the riding club, feeling a little shaken. I knew it was the club right away, because of the smell of horse manure. It's weird, but the only thing that I really like about horses is the smell of their manure. I think it's the only animal that shits something that doesn't stink. A little-known fact. But all I saw were ponies, which surprised me. The kids riding them looked panic stricken. As if it was actually mainly the parents who wanted them to ride, thinking they would enjoy it. There was even a little girl on her mini-horse who was crying. She had a tiny little head and wore a riding helmet. You wanted to take her in your arms to comfort her. Instead, her parents were standing off to the side taking pictures of her. I swear. Parents really are pretty lame a lot of the time.

But Mathilde wasn't there yet. Maybe they hadn't come in from their ride. So I sat down on the bench across the way and waited. You should have seen me: I was stressed out of my mind because of the business with the phone call. But that didn't change anything, I told myself reassuringly. Nobody knew I was here in the park. At one point I stood up to go buy myself something to eat. I wasn't really hungry, even though I hadn't eaten anything all day, but I was bored waiting. There was a guy in a food truck off to one side who made you crêpes, waffles, and stuff like that. What I really would have liked was ice cream. I'm not usually crazy about ice cream, but I felt like having some, I don't know why. I walked over and saw there were four people in line ahead of me. That bummed me out, especially for ice cream, so I went back and sat down. I'd rather wait for Mathilde, and then go buy myself something like that afterward. It would be more fun. But I didn't see anybody coming in from a horseback ride. It was almost ten past five. I was afraid she wasn't coming. Or that I'd made a mistake. But I thought back to the phone call I'd made from my hotel. On the phone, the girl had said there was a reservation in Mathilde's name. So it was fine. Besides, Mathilde had told me the same thing the night before. She went riding every Saturday. All of a sudden I was afraid it might actually be Sunday. A spasm of anxiety went through me, the way you feel on the day of a math test when you realize you've left your calculator at home. But it was Saturday all right, so there was no problem, all I had to do was wait. To pass the time, I started to imagine that to earn money I would buy myself a food truck, too, like the guy across the way. What I would do would be to go to where the schools let out. And I would sell things that people really wanted. Because most of the time the guys who sell you things have no idea what you really want. They sell just anything at all. For example in the métro. All those guys selling posters and stuff. Frankly, it's pathetic. But I couldn't see myself as a vendor, anyway. I'd rather be a writer.

I heard a strange noise behind me in the bushes. I turned around, but I didn't see anything. I was positive there was some sort of animal moving around back there, though, so I took a few steps toward the stream. I didn't know if you were allowed to walk on the grass like that. I didn't think so, but I didn't care. Especially because I heard the noise again, which I was now sure was an animal. I got closer. And just then a totally demented

duck literally leaped out of the water, screaming bloody murder. That duck is crazy, I thought. It scared me. But then I
understood. There was a real tiny duckling on the bank, just a
baby, actually, who didn't know what to do. I thought he was
really, really cute. The mother was thrashing around in the water,
going quack, quack! I couldn't understand why she was getting
so panicky. Then she suddenly flew off, not very high, skim-
ming the water, but in any case she left. I thought she was
really stupid. Anyway, mothers, they always get emotional over
nothing.

At that point, I didn't know what to do next. First I wanted
to go back to my bench, but I thought that maybe the mother
had abandoned the duckling because of me. I felt guilty. And
the little guy was cheeping to break your heart. I was afraid I'd
screwed up by getting so close. I backed up a bit to see if the
mother would come back, but no, she had really packed up and
left, the bitch. So I went back to the duckling and picked him
up in my hands. At first it freaked him out, and then he calmed
down, and I could stroke him very gently. It was crazy. I could
feel his heart beating. And I thought: if I close my hand, I'll crush
him. I wondered what he would do to survive now. But then I
realized that I was probably exaggerating a little. His mother had
just gone to hide. She would certainly come back. It's in the
laws of nature that a mother takes care of her child. If I left the
duckling alone, the mother would be sure to come back in a
minute. So I put him down where I found him, real gently and
all. Then I slipped away and went back to my bench.

After that I went into the club to get some information and not to spend years waiting for nothing. And that's when I saw Mathilde. She was coming out of the stables. It moved me just to see her. I swear. She had already changed her clothes. She wasn't wearing riding pants, at any rate. When our eyes suddenly met, she stopped in her tracks with a tragic look, as if she was trying to understand what the hell I was doing there. Then she smiled, which really reassured me, and came toward me. My heart felt like it was on fire.

"Hi, there."

"Hi. What are you doing here?"

"Oh, nothing. I was in the neighborhood and I thought I'd come see you."

"Oh? That's nice."

"You told me that you went riding in the Bois every Saturday, so I figured this was my chance. I was out for a walk."

"That's funny. Have you ever been to the club before?"

"Not really. I've passed by it, that's all."

"I'd really like to show it to you, but I'm running a little late."

"Oh?"

"Yeah. My father is expecting me."

"Is he here?"

"No, no."

"The horse you ride, what's his name?"

"Titan."

Titan. Horses always have such dumb-ass names.

"Oh, so you have to go?"

"Yeah."

"Mind if I walk you to the entrance?"

"No. If you want."

We walked out of the club side by side, but without saying anything. I didn't know where to begin. Anyway, I was terrified at the idea that she was going to leave at any moment. Her father was expecting her, she'd said. Mathilde gave a little wave to a girl at the front desk. I figured she must've been the one I'd talked to on the phone, from the hotel. Once we were outside, so as not to leave right away, I told Mathilde my story about the duckling. I offered to show him to her, and she agreed. I got it that she really liked animals. I showed her the bushes. When she saw him, she gave a little cry of wonder. That made me happy. "He is soooo cute!" she kept saying.

"How old is he, do you think?"

"I don't know. Probably just a few days."

I got closer, but she shook her head no.

"Don't you want to pick him up?"

"Absolutely not," she answered.

"Why?"

"You mustn't ever do that. Because otherwise you'll leave your smell on him, and then his mother won't recognize him. Picking up a duckling cuts him off from his mother for good. And a duckling without a mother is sure to die."

"Oh, really?"

"Yeah."

What she'd just said really made me feel crappy.

"You're sure?"

"Positive."

Shit, I'd fucked up. But I decided not to tell Mathilde. She would've thought I was really stupid. I made a mental note to take care of the duckling later. We emerged from the bushes and walked toward the kiddie rides.

"So did last night turn out okay?" she asked.

"We wound up not going clubbing with the others."

"Why?"

"I don't like nightclubs that much, you know."

"Me neither."

"We went out for a drink. And then we went home. But really late."

"I wasn't feeling too hot this morning. Especially because I had to help my sister clean everything up. Somebody barfed in the guest bedroom."

"Seriously?"

"Yeah."

"That's gross. You know who it was?"

"No."

We walked by the merry-go-round. I would've liked to suggest we take a spin. Just like that, for fun. And mainly to put off the moment when she would say good-bye to me. But I was afraid she'd think I was immature, so I didn't say anything. Then we started talking about the German teacher. That didn't go particularly well. She also told me a messed-up story about her pen pal, who lived in Berlin or someplace. Mathilde and I were talking because we were afraid of silence, but we weren't saying very important things. I would've liked for us to be telling each other important things, but I didn't know how to go about it. Especially with a girl. Girls are pretty impossible to understand, anyway. I hear that's been scientifically proven.

At times I got a little closer to her. Just a little. Our bodies would touch and it was like electric sparks flew. I thought, oh man . . . But actually we barely brushed each other and besides, it was never on purpose. We wound up in front of the big Dragon ride. I didn't know what else to say, so I asked her if she'd ever ridden it. She said no. So I told her she absolutely had to try it, that she should at least go once before she died. That made her laugh, so I really insisted, and she agreed. I couldn't believe it. But she didn't have any money.

"Don't worry," I said. "My treat."

I ran to the place where you buy tickets and bought a whole book of them. It was really expensive, but I didn't care. If need be, I would have given all my money just to be with her for a while. Then I came running back. For people who don't know anything about anything, I'll say that the Dragon is a kind of roller coaster, but Chinese. Mathilde was wearing a big smile. I swear. I think it amused her to see me running all over for something that was supposed to be for children. In short, she looked excited. Me too, for that matter. We sat down in the car together. Two kids got in behind us. They looked to be about ten. I think they were brothers; they sort of looked like each other. The smaller one wasn't able to put on his seatbelt, so I helped him. Then a bell rang. And the beast started to move.

"It seems that some people died on this ride last year," I told Mathilde as we were starting.

"No, really?"

"I swear. Some guys fell out when it went upside down."

"Are you kidding me?"

"Yeah."

She started to laugh, but right away her laugh turned into a shout because we suddenly shot down an incredibly steep drop. The two kids behind us started yelling too. It was more than shouting, it was screaming. So I started in, too. As loud as I could. That did the trick, and the four of us were like hysterics who couldn't stop screaming. We were going so fast, we couldn't see anything anymore. Our hair stuck out in every direction. Especially Mathilde's, seeing as how it was a lot longer than mine. Our speed was really off the charts. The worst part was the final curve: it was banked so steeply that your stomach turned upside down, or at least whatever was in it. But that wasn't the end yet. We passed the starting place and right away set out for another lap. After a while, when you got used to the speed and all, it became almost pleasant. It was a little like opening a car window on the highway and sticking your head out. All that pressure on your face, it made you crazy. It was freedom, whereas we were everywhere in chains. But after a while, you felt like you were flying, I swear. That's what I yelled to Mathilde, for that matter: "We're flying! We're flying!" Our yells were turning into laughs, and vice versa. Then we were nearly at the death turn, the final one. Going at top speed. It was scary. And as she screamed louder and louder, Mathilde took my hand. Like someone who's afraid and is looking for something to comfort her. Except that I felt that the fear was just an excuse to hold my hand. And she hadn't done what she did as a reflex, but like something she'd been thinking about doing for the past few minutes. I couldn't believe it. Even I would never have dared do that. Girls, sometimes they kill you.

In the death turn I screamed with happiness.

Then the car slowed down and stopped completely. She immediately took her hand away. We left the Dragon, pretending like nothing had happened. But I could still feel the pressure of her fingers there, in my palm. And even though I've done lots of things with girls, even sexual things, at that moment, I can tell you, I thought it was the most exciting thing that had ever happened in my life. I swear.

Chapter 17

We weren't sure what to do next, so I suggested that we buy something to eat. Suddenly Mathilde didn't seem to be in a hurry anymore. We went over to one of the food trucks. She got a crêpe. So did I. We sat down on a bench. We stayed like that for a long time, and it was almost the definition of happiness, but it was much more fragile than a definition; you couldn't have written it down and put it in the dictionary like something definite that everybody agrees on. On the contrary, it was as fragile as a soap bubble. The least little sentence could burst it.

"I have to go now," said Mathilde.

"You're meeting your father, right?"

"Yeah. We're going shopping. I promised him. What time is it?"

"I'm going home in a taxi. I can drop you off, if you like. You'll save time."

She looked surprised. We didn't usually take taxis, at our age.

"That works for me," she finally said.

I would have loved to go to the movies with her, but I didn't know how to ask her. She'd held my hand, though. When a girl holds your hand, that's a sign, isn't it? Also, I was afraid that she might say yes, but for next week. Right then, next Saturday seemed as far away as the last page of the calendar. A pigeon walked over to us, and Mathilde tore off a bit of her crêpe and tossed it to it. The very next moment, there were four or five of them. Personally, I hate pigeons. If it was up to me, I think I'd exterminate them all. Throw stones at their ugly mugs. Damn. I couldn't wait. In a week, I might be at Les Roches Noires, for all I knew, or in Italy. One thing was for sure, I wouldn't be hiding out in Paris anymore.

"Do you know anything about Italy?" I asked her.

"I went to Rome once."

"Was it nice?"

"Not bad. Why?"

"Because I may have to go there."

"To Italy?"

"Yeah."

"That's great. Why?"

I don't know why—it was probably because of the unusual situation and all, the way I was feeling, and the fact that she took my hand during the Dragon ride—but I started to tell her what had been happening to me. Skipping the details, of course; I've read Balzac. But I gave her a summary of my mother's marriage. Of Bénédicte, who hated me. Of the fact that I was completely alone. On the loose. Running away. I told her everything. She listened to it all in silence. I honestly wondered what she would think about the whole story. When I was finished, she just asked:

"Do you think you're going to go home?"

"I can't anymore."

"Think so?"

"Yeah. It's impossible. It's too late."

"But you're going to get caught sooner or later."

"I know. That's why I'd like to see Italy first."

As I told her all that, a wave of feelings went through me. I could feel my chin start to tremble. But I controlled myself, and I don't think she noticed. In any case, she sat there for a long time without saying anything. Then she stood up. I thought I was going to die. And we started walking toward the park entrance. I followed her, of course. I was afraid I'd screwed up by telling her the truth. But as we walked along, she told me a story. Apparently her sister Emilie had also run away a lot at one point. Especially during vacations. According to Mathilde, something unusual happened four years ago, before her parents got divorced. They had all gone to Île de Ré together on a family trip. They stayed in a hotel. The two sisters slept in one room and the parents in another. In those days, their father was much stricter than he was now. He and Emilie weren't getting along at all. Especially because he wouldn't let her go out at night, which all her friends were allowed to do. So she would often join them secretly, after midnight. Mathilde didn't know about it, because Emilie would wait for her to fall asleep before she left. She was sneaking out, in other words. This happened in

July. The place where everybody went dancing was called La Pergola. It was a nightclub, but open air. What happened was that one night Mathilde woke up in the middle of the night and saw that Emilie wasn't there. She started to freak out. She first thought something had happened to her. She waited for a while, to see if she would come back. And then, because she didn't know what else to do, and also because she was ten years old, she went and knocked on her parents' bedroom door. And that's when the drama began. Their father got dressed, took the car, and made the rounds of the nightclubs. He was absolutely furious. And of course he eventually walked into La Pergola, correctly figuring he would find Emilie there. And he wasn't wrong.

Emilie was dancing when she caught sight of him. It must have been a shock to see her father looking for her. She thought he was sleeping peacefully back at the hotel. It was probably the shock of her life. She barely had enough time to run and hide in the toilet before he saw her. But her father recognized some of his daughter's friends, and asked them where she was. They all said they didn't know. Real friends, in other words. The opposite of Marco. If he'd been in their place he would've said: "She's hiding in the toilet, it's in back on the right, and if you want her new cell number, here it is." But they lied, and the father believed Emilie wasn't in the club. So when he finally went back to the hotel, he was in a panic, imagining everything that could have happened to his oldest daughter. He waited in the bedroom all night long. Mathilde had never seen her father like that, he was so stressed. For her part, Emilie didn't dare go home anymore, since she knew she'd been busted. "I'm going to get killed," she probably said to herself. And she wasn't wrong.

In this story at least, nobody was wrong.

One of Emilie's girlfriends offered to let her sleep at her place, and she accepted for the first night. But the next morning, it was the same story. She didn't dare go back, and the more time went by, the less she dared. The father went to the cops, who launched an investigation, especially since a girl had been raped at Île de Ré the year before. Things were starting to spiral out of control. Plus, the girlfriend told her that she had to leave, so Emilie spent the next night sleeping on the beach. Next morning after that, she returned to the hotel in tears. Her hair was all dirty, and she felt ashamed. But the moment her father saw her, instead of yelling or slapping her as you might expect, he threw his arms around her and kissed her. He called her "my darling." He even cried as he hugged her, saying, "Don't ever do that to me again." According to Mathilde, it was from then on that Emilie and her father began to get along. And even to love each other.

I wondered why Mathilde was telling me this story. Maybe it was to say that I was wrong when I said I couldn't go home again. To say that, contrary to what I thought, no one would kill me on the spot. That's possible. Unless you knew my mother, who is really hard and strict and all. You'd really have trouble imagining her crying and hugging you and saying nice things to you.

"So what are you going to do?" asked Mathilde.

"I don't know."

"Where are you sleeping?"

"In a hotel."

I pulled a sheet of paper out of my pocket, as if I needed proof. She looked at it. It was quai Voltaire letterhead stationery. She thought a moment longer, then said:

"Do you have enough money?"

I was about to tell her that I'd stolen François's credit card, but stopped myself at the last moment. Maybe that was something I should keep to myself.

"I'm getting by."

So we were finally talking about important things, and it felt really good. The problem was, we'd reached the Jardin entrance. In life, things we think are beautiful never last long enough. It made me heartsick to think that soon I would say good-bye to Mathilde without knowing if I would ever see her again, or what. An available taxi was waiting right at the entrance. Like an irony of fate. But we had barely gotten in when Mathilde gave a little shriek like a marmot's.

"What's the matter?" I asked.

"I forgot my purse."

"Where?"

"At the club. Rats! I left it in the stall. I'll have to go back."

"Can't you get it next time?"

"No, it's important. This is so dumb of me! My wallet's in it."

"Wait, stay in the taxi. I'll run back. It won't take me a minute."

216 · FLORIAN ZELLER

"You sure?"

"No problem."

The truth is, I was happy to do her the favor. Besides, I really liked the idea that a girl would be waiting for me in a taxi at the entrance to the Bois de Boulogne. I got out of the taxi. I explained to the girl at the ticket booth, the rodent, that I'd left my things inside, and she let me through. Then I started running like a madman. I tried to imagine what Mathilde might have in her purse. A pair of panties, for all I knew. I couldn't believe all the extraordinary adventures that were happening to me. I got to the club. Mathilde had said it was in Titan's stall.

Titan.

I asked the girl where the stalls were. She pointed vaguely. A moment later, I was searching the names of the horses. *Titan*. I opened the stall. Luckily it was empty. Right away I spotted Mathilde's purse on the hay off to one side. I scooped it up— child's play. Then I suddenly felt a hand on my shoulder, which really startled me. I turned around.

It was Bénédicte.

I practically had a heart attack, she so freaked me out. The bitch was wearing riding clothes. And in that split second I realized she belonged to the club, too. Damn!

"What the hell are you doing here, Julien?"

"Nothing."

I must have looked all pale. I could feel the color of fear settling on my face.

"Where were you? Everybody's worried! Are you stupid, or what? Why did you disappear that way? Your mother's going out of her mind. Where'd you spend the night?"

She walked toward me, and I backed up against the wall. I was caught, like in a trap.

"Don't come near me."

"You have to go home now."

She was giving me a murderous look.

"Don't come near me, I'm telling you."

"What are you doing here at the club?"

I almost said, "I came to see you." But I was in no mood for jokes.

"Leave me alone. Let me by."

I tried to push her aside, but she resisted.

"No. You're staying here. I'm calling the parents."

"You do that, and I'll kill you."

"Don't you get it?"

"You're the one who doesn't get anything."

"You little shit."

"Get out of the way."

I shoved her, but she hung onto me like a lunatic. I swear. She wouldn't let go of my sleeve. Then she hit me with her crop, which she had in her other hand. As if I were a horse. It hurt like hell. I backed away. I could feel the trap closing on me. Damn. And to think that Mathilde was waiting for me in a taxi not two minutes from here! I tried to calm down, in spite of the rage she had aroused in me.

"All right, are you happy now? You hit me with your crop. Do you feel better?"

"You're really crazy, Julien."

"Sure, sure."

"Anyway, it's like I've always said, you'll wind up like your father. With the nut jobs."

Bénédicte's usual refrain was to hint that my father hadn't died of cancer, as my mother had told me, but that he was in an asylum. I knew perfectly well that it was totally false, but at that moment it made me crazy. So I shoved her again, to get by. She screamed at the top of her lungs. Then she hit me again with her crop, partly on my face. It felt like she broke the skin or something. In any case it hurt incredibly bad. And I could tell that she was about to do it again. She could have gone on hitting me like that until I was quiet and they could handcuff me. So to make her let me go and stop alerting everybody by screaming, I punched her in the nose, really hard. It worked. She fell down. And she sat like that, without moving, sobbing and holding her nose, which was bleeding. I snatched up her crop and raised it as if I was about to hit her. To be honest, I came within an inch of doing it. I said: "Go ahead, repeat what you just said. Repeat it!" I could hear myself breathing, it was like an animal, a racehorse, nervous and all, my nostrils were completely dilated. I had to make an effort not to hit her, because I could feel I was this close to slashing at her. In the end, I lowered my arm and just added: "Now you're going to leave me in peace. Okay? You're going to let me live in peace."

She was still bawling. She turned to me. She couldn't even speak a normal sentence, everything was so mixed up: her blood, her breathing, her gasps, her sobs, her insults. She looked pitiful. And then she started up again: "You're going to wind up in an asylum, with your father. Because that's where he is, your psychopath of a father." That I couldn't stand. I punched her in the face again. Something snapped. I was afraid I'd hit her too hard. That I'd really messed up her face. I thought of calling for someone. Or helping her up. But I just left. Out of fear. I could hear screams behind me. Louder and louder. Terrible screams. Like a woman giving birth and being torn in two by the pain.

After that, I began running, running, running. I didn't know you could run so fast. And the more I ran the more I realized what I'd just done. Damn. I'd gone overboard. The taxi was waiting. I climbed in, and right away told the driver to head for the Champs-Élysées. Mathilde was looking at me strangely. I must have looked pretty scary, or something.

"What's the matter?"

"Nothing, nothing."

I turned around to look through the window to see if anyone was following me. Nobody was there. My heart was pounding at top speed. As if I'd killed someone. I swear, it was the same feeling. Unfortunately, the taxi was hemmed in. The car in front of us was blocking our way.

"Step on it," I said.

I turned around again. This time I saw two guys running toward us.

"Shit!"

"What's going on, Julien?"

"What the hell's wrong with that car?"

"Hey, I can't drive over it," said the stupid driver.

"It's nothing," I told Mathilde with a phony reassuring smile, as I handed her her purse.

But I could see her looking at my fist. And then my cheek, which stung a little. She saw the blood.

"Did you hurt yourself? What happened to you?"

"I'll tell you later."

Slowly, the car in front of us began to move. Turns out the woman was trying to park, but she was driving like a jackass.

"Honk your horn!"

"What good'll that do?"

Behind us, the two guys were coming out of the park. One of them looked in my direction. It freaked me out. So I bent down and put my head on Mathilde's knees. She turned around and saw the two guys. I think she understood.

"You can get by now," she told the driver.

"Just a second."

The car in front of us couldn't get into the parking space, so the woman gave up, which finally cleared the way. I sat up as we started to drive off. I could see the two guys looking everywhere, right and left, but they became smaller and smaller until they didn't exist anymore. I swear, I'm not making this up. That's how it happened.

Chapter 18

I calmed down a little as we rode along, but I had no idea what to do next. You have to understand that this whole thing happened at top speed. Here, I'm taking my time telling you about it and all, but in real life it happened super fast—no time to catch your breath or anything. The excitement gradually settled down, like motes of dust. The driver turned on the radio. I gave Mathilde a fake smile. She looked at me questioningly. I wasn't at all sure I should tell her the truth. I didn't much want to, even though I realized that she would find out about it anyway, since what had just happened would be the talk of the club. She would know everything in a week at the most, and would think I was an animal. I felt a little ashamed. Still, Bénédicte had blocked my way, and she'd whipped me across the face. That girl is a public menace. I ran my hand over my cheek, which still stung. I could tell I had a cut. Thinking back on all that now, it seems weird that I never suspected Bénédicte might belong to the same club as Mathilde. I imagined her being at that other club I'd gone to with her a couple of times in the very beginning, and I didn't remember it being in the Bois de Boulogne. In short, I hadn't been careful.

For Mathilde, I launched into a cock and bull story. I first thought to tell her that just as I got to Titan's stall, I saw a guy with her purse open who was about to steal it. He wouldn't give it up, so I had to fight him. That wasn't too believable, and as I started telling it, I had another idea—a much better one, really unbeatable. I said that on the way, I ran into a guy I'd been dreaming of catching up with for years, namely Yann Chevillard. I swear. I had to explain that he was someone who really put me through the wringer when I was an adolescent, at age ten or eleven. He'd been so sadistic with me in those days, there were times when I wanted to die. No kidding. So when I recognized Chevillard, I couldn't resist: I yelled to him, to make sure it was really him, and when he turned around, I gave him the biggest punch of my life. As a souvenir for the past, if you like. He was tough, though, and that didn't do the trick, especially since he had a riding crop in his hand—he was coming out of the club. So we really fought, like Achilles against Hector. A fistfight worthy of an R-rated movie, I told her.

Mathilde looked convinced. So was I, for that matter. As I was telling her all this, I almost began to believe it was the truth. An intense joy rose up in me, as if after all these years I had finally paid Chevillard back for the humiliations he and his pals had inflicted on me. It had taken me a long time, but I was coming out of it with my head high. I'd taken my revenge, but not with a bad feeling or anything. Just with the idea of fixing what he had damaged. Rendering justice, in other words. I actually felt as if all that were true. Today, I think it probably was the truth, except that Bénédicte had served as a stand-in, and that somewhere in my soul, the punch I gave her was actually meant for Yann Chevillard.

We drove the length of the avenue, the one that leads directly to the Place de l'Étoile. Having told my story, I felt like a hero. It couldn't have been better in a dream. Even though I was still feeling the shock of what I'd just done in reality, and my body was secretly shaking. My consolation was sensing that Mathilde was pretty impressed. I had gotten all my self-confidence back. If I'd had to, I could've made her believe that the Unknown Soldier buried at the Place de l'Étoile was actually my father. I swear. At that moment, the difference between truth and lying didn't matter anymore. It was a meaningless boundary now. The only thing that mattered was that I was in a taxi with Mathilde, that we were within a few inches of each other, and that she had taken my hand, earlier.

Once on the Champs, she pulled out the sheet of paper I'd given her and she read it aloud.

"Hôtel du Quai Voltaire. Why there?"

"No reason."

"Do you have TV in your room?"

"No, but I hate TV anyway. They're all jerks on TV."

The driver, who was really a pain in the ass, interrupted: "How far along on the Champs?"

"Rue Pierre-Charron," answered Mathilde.

"We're almost there."

"I know."

I spotted the pizzeria of the night before. It made me nostalgic, as if I was remembering something from a really long time ago.

"It would make me really sad if we weren't able to see each other again," I dared tell her.

She thought for a long time. "Were you serious when you said you wanted to go to Italy?"

"I think so, yeah."

"And when would you leave?"

"Tomorrow, for all I know."

"As soon as tomorrow?"

I took my courage in both hands.

"Do you think we could see each other later, after you go shopping?"

Again she thought for a long time. I told her that we could go to the movies, for example. Or anywhere. She said she would try, since it would be the only way for us to see each other. But first she had to work it out with her father.

"It'd be best not to tell him that we ran into each other," I said.

I knew that my mother would be conducting a little back-door investigation. She wasn't the kind to twiddle her thumbs waiting for me to come home. For all I knew, she had already alerted Mathilde's father. I had been last seen at his place, after all. So we had to be really careful. Mathilde said it wasn't a problem. Her father didn't mind her going out. He wasn't the kind to throw his weight around.

"We can just meet at my hotel. That would be the simplest."

"What time?"

"I don't know. Let's say nine o'clock."

"That works for me," she said at last with a wonderful smile.

"What number?" asked the driver.

I would've gladly eliminated the damn driver from the scene for you.

"Number 13."

"Then we're here. It's right there."

"I'm going on," I told him.

Mathilde looked me in the eyes for a long time. When a girl you love looks at you like that, it can kill you right on the spot. Then she asked for my cell number, in case there was a problem, and keyed it into her phone's memory. That was a really good sign, I told myself. After that, she ran off, like a deer. I didn't know what else to think, except that I was crazy in love. That had already happened to me, of course, but not like this.

The day was taking an incredible turn, if you thought about it. I was really nervous at the idea of seeing her again that night, but also really excited. And in a hotel, too. I couldn't believe it. I ran my hand over my cheek again. It stung terribly.

I told the driver to take me to my hotel. On the way I imagined what must have happened at the club after I left, and it made me want to puke. But I figured they must have lots of stuff on hand to patch up Bénédicte's snotty little face. Girls who ride horses often get hurt, because of falls. The club probably had an incredible first-aid kit for cases much more serious than an enormous punch in the nose. For all I knew, I'd broken it. I mean the bone. Otherwise she wouldn't have bled so much. I hope not, I told myself. Speaking of first aid, Bénédicte once told me a story about something I think actually happened. A girl at her club was picking something up off the ground when a horse stepped right on her hand and cut off one of her fingers. I don't know if you can imagine that. She screamed like hell. They took her to the hospital right away. But what was sort of gross was that the club manager told everybody they had to find the piece of finger, which had to be somewhere in the mud. You can sew them back on, apparently. So all the girls in the club got down and started looking for the fingertip, and the person who found it was Bénédicte.

I'm telling you all this as a way of saying that I wasn't too worried about her nose. They would take care of it right there. On the other hand, she must have called the parents. I could already imagine my mother's reaction. Remember, she said that I was becoming a delinquent when she realized I smoked cigarettes. So now if she learned that I'd beaten up my fake stepsister, she might turn me into the police herself. In any case, they would really have it in for me after this. Especially François, considering that the punch I gave his daughter was a really hard one. To tell you the truth, I would never have believed I could throw such hard punches. But it's not as if I made up my mind to do what I did. It just happened in the moment. If I'd asked myself, "Do you want to punch her?" for example, I would certainly have answered no. It just sort of went off by itself, because of what she said about my father. But in the beginning, I certainly hadn't planned to bust her nose, believe me. Because when you think about it, busting your sister's nose is really something. When you say it like that, it's scary. In fact, I was a violent guy. I'd never thought it, but all of a sudden I realized I was a violent guy.

The driver dropped me off across from my hotel. My stomach was starting to ache because I hadn't eaten anything all day, except for the crêpe, earlier. Yet I wasn't at all hungry, far from it. That's why I didn't want to go buy myself something to eat. On the other hand, I wanted a pack of cigarettes. So instead of going into the hotel, I walked around the neighborhood in search of a bistro that sold them. I was really feeling stressed. Finding a bistro was taking forever, because the neighborhood was lousy with art galleries. All you saw in the windows were paintings,

paintings, and more paintings, but never any cigarettes. I finally located a sort of Maison de la Presse. I went in, and since there were some people at the cash register, I started by checking out the magazines. It occurred to me that it might be smart to buy a few, since I had a lot of time to kill. I took a look at what was available, which I can sum up this way: an embarrassment of riches. I chose *Entrevue*. The cover showed a fairly attractive, almost naked girl, with this written underneath: "What Women Want." Okay. That was educational, sort of. Off to one side was something I would've liked to buy for myself: a *Life and Times of Scrooge McDuck*. I know, I know. I'm fourteen years old, and obviously, I'm really too old for that. I'm well aware of it. And I'm not stupid, either. Walking up to the cash register with a *Scrooge McDuck* isn't the coolest thing to do. The sales-girl would take me for a retard. And if there's something I can't stand, it's being taken for a retard. If I showed up at the register with a *Scrooge McDuck*, the girl could never imagine that the guy in front of her just happened to have a date with a girl in a hotel that evening. And that he was dangerous, too.

In a Maison de la Presse, there are two things that are hard for a guy my age to buy: a *Scrooge McDuck* and a skin magazine. Taking care not to attract too much attention, I discreetly wandered over to the adult section. I felt like I'd found a gold mine. My theory is that it really takes guts to dare take one of those magazines to the girl at the register. Because the girl is going to look at you sideways, and in her eyes it's obvious that you're a disgusting, filthy pervert. But just between us, I don't see what's so disgusting about glancing at one of those magazines from time to time. But, hey, what's tricky is being able to look at them without everybody catching you. My dream would be to take a good look at all those magazines once and for all. Just to confirm that I'm not interested. Because the truth is, and I want to make this clear to all my female readers, those kinds of magazines don't really interest me. In fact not all. I swear. Even if you do have to check them out from time to time just to be sure.

In the end I went to the register and asked for a pack of menthols. Just like that. I'm not crazy about mentholated cigarettes. Besides, several people have told me they make you sterile. But I've also heard that they're the least likely to give you bad breath. I had a date with Mathilde, remember, and where breath was concerned, I wanted to be at my best, if you know what I mean. So I put the cigarettes on the counter, then my magazines. Self-confident, like. First *Entrevue*, the magazine with the naked girl on the cover. Then *Scrooge McDuck* on top, to hide it. And to top it all off, so as not to be taken for a kid retard, I asked the girl if they had *Le Monde*. They did, as it happens. It was off to one side. I snatched a copy and put in on top of the stack.

"Will that be all?" the girl asked me.

Chapter 19

I brought all that back to the hotel. On the way I switched on my cell to see what time it was. I knew it would be quite a while before Mathilde showed up, but I wanted to check. The phone rang right away. Damn. Some things in life are just a drag. It was my voicemail. I listened to the beginning—"You have four new messages . . ."—then I hung up. Honestly, I had no intention of listening to them. My mother was probably threatening to kill me. And Marco was probably wondering why I hadn't shown up at the Marché. Too bad for him; he'd have a long wait. I bet that prick hadn't even bothered to go there. He must've figured the cops would have picked me up or something. As a matter of fact, all the people looking for me weren't that far away: just four or five streets from there. I switched my phone off again so as not to think about that.

The guy at the front desk was the same one I'd seen a little earlier, the one who'd mistaken me for a girl—from the back, I should point out. He gave me a shit-eating grin and he asked if I'd had a good day. I said, "Incredible." But he was staring at

me oddly, and I figured it was because of the cut on my face.
Judging by his expression, it must not have looked too good. I
quickly took my key and went upstairs. Once in my room, I lit
myself a menthol cigarette, using the hotel's matches. What I
like about hotels is that they always put out tons of matchbooks
everywhere, and that's not counting the ashtrays. Then I went
to rinse my face. I was pretty well cut up, and it was stinging
more and more. After that, I stretched out on my bed to think
about what I would do to get ready for the evening. Then I
picked up the room phone and asked Information for train res-
ervations. I was connected and got an SNCF operator almost
right away. What I wanted was the schedule of trains to Italy.
The woman asked me my destination. At random, I said,
"Rome." She looked it up on her computer, then asked when
I wanted to leave. I said, "Around noon tomorrow." Turned
out there was a train at 12:20 p.m. from the Gare de Lyon with
a change at Lausanne, then a sleeper to Rome. "That's perfect,"
I said, and wrote the departure information on the hotel notepad.
Twenty past noon, Gare de Lyon. She offered to book my ticket
online, but I didn't want her to. I no longer had a credit card,
in any case. And I would never have done it anyway—I didn't
want it traced.

I opened the minibar to see what there was. But it was a
mini-minibar: where champagne was concerned, it was pretty
stingy. So I went downstairs to order a bottle and two glasses.
Champagne glasses, I specified. To be put on my room bill. The
guy promised he would bring it all up. I just love hotels. Then

I went back to my room, feeling more and more relaxed. But at the same time, more and more nervous at the idea that I would soon be with Mathilde again. In barely an hour and a half. I thought back to the night before, which I'd spent outside, walking without knowing where I was going. It had been pretty dismal, compared to the one ahead of me. I opened my *Entrevue*. Okay girls, tell me everything: What do they like to have done to them? I scanned every page for the answer to the question raised on the cover. There were mostly a lot of girls who were naked, but casually. Not in a dirty way, I mean. But as for getting an answer, forget it. Anyway, I don't see how someone could tell you what to do to a girl. Because first of all, it depends on the girl, and it also depends on her age. I'm sure there are things that some girls like and others don't, for example. That's why you shouldn't try to understand them, in my opinion. I don't understand anything about girls. All I know is that they understand us really well. Which isn't too hard, actually.

Suddenly somebody knocked on the door. I tensed up. Right away, I thought of my mother and I hid the magazine under my pillow. That was lame, I admit, but hey. I went to open the door. It was the guy from the bar, bringing up the bottle. He'd thought to put it in a bucket with ice and everything. It was really something else. And two champagne glasses, just like I'd asked him. He set all that on the desk. I thanked him again and again, and promised myself to remember him in terms of tips before leaving France. Then I went back to my reading. But the truth is, *Entrevue* wasn't nearly as good as *Scrooge*

McDuck. So I ran a bath, and when the tub was nice and full I slipped into it with my comic book. What I like best is the big centerfold adventure, with Scrooge McDuck, Donald Duck, and Huey, Dewey, and Louie. And the two Beagle Boys burglars who can never do anything right. Idiots, in other words. It cracked me up. I don't know why, but reading that in the tub made me happy. It's not my fault, I'm sentimental.

When I got out, the water was cold and I had finished reading. This time, I'd insisted on having soap; you never know. Then I put the clothes I'd worn earlier back on. It wasn't too sharp that Mathilde had already seen me dressed that way last night and again this afternoon. She would probably think I never changed my clothes. But at the same time she knew about my unusual situation. There were extenuating circumstances. I carefully hid my *Scrooge McDuck* and *Entrevue* in the closet, and put *Le Monde* on the table, well in evidence. Then I opened the window for some fresh air. I took the occasion to smoke another cigarette while looking at the Louvre. My face still hurt, which made me think back to that creep Yann Chevillard and the fight to the death we'd had on his building landing . . . And suddenly I got the idea of checking with Information, to see. The bastard was probably still living with his parents, so I just asked for "Monsieur Chevillard." They gave me three addresses in Paris. He must live at one of the three, for sure. I wrote them down without quite knowing why. Someday, I would find him and make him pay, I told myself. I closed my eyes, and imagined myself beating him up. Yann Chevillard would suffer, because I was a violent guy. But I was mainly saying that to say it to myself. I knew perfectly well I would never do it. I didn't give a damn about Yann Chevillard now. He was part of another life. Part of that time when I'd really been tormented by idiots.

I turned on my cell to check the time. The voicemail rang again. This time I had five messages. I was afraid that Mathilde had left the last one. No kidding. So I decided to listen to it, but only after systematically skipping the others. On the fifth, I recognized my mother's voice. I barely gave her enough time to say my name before erasing the message by pressing the 2 button. I didn't even want to hear the sound of her voice. I was too afraid of what I would hear. She must know all about the business with Bénédicte. But oddly enough, I was relieved that the message was from her. My worst nightmare would have been for Mathilde to cancel for some reason. It was nearly eight thirty.

As I lay on my bed, I imagined her getting ready. I don't know if you've noticed, but girls are really careful about how they look. Sometimes too much. I figured Mathilde wouldn't show up wearing the same clothes as before. That's why I could visualize her in front of her mirror, trying on various dresses. And checking to see which bra made her chest look nicest, for all I knew. I don't know if I already told you this, but girls' chests practically drive me crazy.

I switched on my cell: eight thirty-six. I switched it back off.

Then I thought about Italy again. The first person ever to tell me about Italy was Madame Morozvitch. She said she'd lived there for quite a few years because of her husband, who worked at something or other, but in Italy. What I'd like would be to go down to the coast not far from Capri, if you see what I mean. I could easily find a way to earn a little money. And I would stay there, where the weather is always nice. As I thought about all that, I got the idea of going to see Madame Morozvitch. She was in a nursing home near Versailles. I wondered if you could visit her on Sunday. Probably yes, since families were mainly free on the weekend to visit their parents. Even though I'd heard that most of the time they didn't go to see them very often. Nursing homes are set up for just that reason, which makes me really sad. If push came to shove I'd find death more attractive than the hallways of some nursing home. In any case, when it's my turn I hope I'll have the guts to check out before I turn into a vegetable in a wrinkle ranch that smells of piss.

My cell said it was eight forty.

I got off the bed and sat down at the desk. I'd just had an idea. I wouldn't actually have time to visit the nursing home, since my train was at twelve twenty and I probably wasn't going to get up at the crack of dawn. There was no point in stopping by for just two minutes. Especially since Versailles isn't right next door. The best thing would be to write her something. So I sat down at my table, pushed *Le Monde* aside, and started to write

Madame Morozvitch that I was leaving for Italy and also to thank her for teaching me to love books and all. Basically, she'd been the nicest person in this whole business. For a long time I considered telling her that I owed her quite a lot of money. I even thought of taking some of what I had left and sending it to her. That way at least I would have settled all my accounts before leaving. But I knew very well I wouldn't do it. It was just to entertain the idea, to give me the feeling I'd thought of it. Anyway, it's too risky to send money through the mail. I know a guy who got ripped off that way. Honestly, mail carriers don't miss a trick. Before they deliver a letter, they always hold it up to the sunlight, to see if they can spot any cash inside. Everyone knows that. Take a bill and put it in an envelope. If you mail it, you're sure to never see it again. So I couldn't pay Madame Morozvitch back. She wouldn't be able to use the money in her nursing home anyway. I bet her son would get it all. Thanks, but no thanks. That one really is an asshole. He doesn't know how lucky he is to have Madame Morozvitch for a mother. He should spend three days at my place, and he'd see. I reread my letter several times. It really moved me. Because I was saying good-bye as if I would never see her again. I imagined an entire volume of my correspondence, and the first letter, the first page, would be the one I'd just written to say good-bye to Madame Morozvitch. Then I went downstairs because it was almost time for Mathilde.

There wasn't anybody in the bar, but from the little I'd seen, there was never anybody in that bar. The TV was on. I asked the bartender for something to drink. I figured I could order whatever I wanted, since they'd already imprinted the credit card when I arrived. They had no reason to be suspicious. So if I asked for something, they would agree, without wondering whether I was ripping them off or anything. All they wanted from me in exchange was a signature. No problem. That's why I could order even the most expensive stuff, like my bottle of champagne, earlier. I imagined the impression that would make on Mathilde. In the meantime, I ordered some apricot juice, because I like that better. The bartender gave me a friendly smile. I stayed at the bar. Obviously, I couldn't wait for Mathilde right in my room. That would be a bit much. The technique was to meet here at the bar, and then discuss what she felt like doing for the evening. I was sorry I hadn't bought an *Officiel des spectacles*, to know what movies were playing. But we could just walk around and look. There are usually hundreds of showings around ten o'clock. We would see when we got there. And for all I knew maybe she wouldn't feel like going to the movies.

Eight forty-six.

The guy brought me my juice, but I wound up asking him for a glass of champagne, too. I'm not crazy about champagne, to tell you the truth. What I especially like is the idea of drinking it. That's the best, I think. But as a general rule I practically never drink it. I prefer apricot juice or wine. I hate beer. Anyway, I started sipping my juice. The guy, who was pretty nice, gave me a little plate of crackers. I asked him where the nearest movie theaters were. He said the best thing was to go to Odéon; you've got all the movies you want there. Then I wondered if maybe Mathilde wouldn't rather go to a restaurant so we could have a cozy dinner together. In that case I would have to come up with a sort of fancy place. Not at all like a pizzeria. More the sort of place where they have you taste the wine before pouring you a full glass of it. That's real style, I think. But I'm sure that would bore her. A movie was better, and besides, it would be dark. After that we could walk back in the night, and I would suggest we drink a last glass of champagne in my room. She might hesitate, as a matter of form and because she's a girl. So I would tell her right away that it didn't commit her to anything, it was just so I could spend a little more time with her, and then she would say yes.

There was a series of stupid things on the TV: commercials, then the weather, then lots of boring stuff. I always wondered who they were, the millions of people who watch TV every evening. Judging by what you see on television, I think housewives' brains are clinically dead. I swear: clinically dead. For example, there's a commercial where a girl tells you that she put this cream on her skin, and since then, her face has really changed. You really have to be a moron to believe that. Because for sure this girl never heard of the cream before doing the commercial. It's just that she was offered a lot of money to tell housewives that. So right away the housewife thinks: if this girl says it, it must be true. So she buys the cream the next week and puts it all over her face. Except that it would still look like a housewife's face. No cream is going to change that. It's obvious. So when you see the girl on TV saying she looks ten years younger now that she's started using this cream, you figure that television people must really think housewives are idiots. And you mainly figure they're probably right, since they've done studies right and left to know what to say. It's depressing. I turned on my cell. I still had the same worry in the pit of my stomach. I didn't have any messages. That reassured me a lot. Mathilde would have warned me if she'd been held up. Given the time, she must already be on her way over. So there was no more risk of her canceling on me. I was sorry I hadn't asked for her cell number. I would have sent her a text message. In the meantime I fiddled with my phone to change the ringtone, which was really too crappy.

At one point, I heard the ding! of the front door. I stood up. She was here. It was time.

Unfortunately, it wasn't her, but a man who walked right into the bar, greeted the guy behind the counter, and went to sit at a table near the window. The bartender turned off the TV, and put on music instead. Sort of jazz. Then he fixed a tall glass— whiskey, I think—and brought it to the man who had come in. Looking at him, I felt I'd seen him before somewhere. He looked sad. Given the setting, I figured he was a regular, and that he always drank the same thing every time. That was convenient. The bartender didn't even have to ask him what he wanted anymore.

"Care for another?" he asked me.

In the meantime, I had drunk my glass of champagne, almost without realizing it. The bartender wanted to serve me another one. I preferred not. I hold my liquor very well, but I practically hadn't eaten anything all day, so I said no thanks. At that, the bartender sort of leaned over the counter, to get closer. He noticed that I was interested in the guy at the table, since all I'd done was to watch him since he came in. So he started telling me about him. And he told me a sort of mind-blowing thing, I think. According to him, the guy's name was Monsieur Elme. He came there every evening, and he stayed really late. But the main thing was, he put away an incredible number of drinks. Sometimes as many as ten whiskeys. His technique for knowing when to stop was that after each drink he would pull a photograph from his breast pocket. He would look at it for a long time. And afterward, he would either order another drink, or he would go home. So of course I asked the bartender what the picture was. And he looked pleased, because that was exactly the question he wanted me to ask. He said he'd wondered the same thing, so one day he asked the guy straight out about the photo that he always looked at between two drinks. And the guy told him: "It's a picture of my wife. When she looks beautiful, I go home."

That made the bartender laugh. But I couldn't tell if it was a joke that he told every customer or if it was really the truth. And I couldn't have cared less, to be honest. I was worried because Mathilde still wasn't there. So I stood up. I could tell that if I stayed, the bartender would go on telling me stories like that, and I wasn't in the mood. So I went back upstairs.

In my room, I started reading *Entrevue* again. It was nine fifteen, but it wasn't surprising that Mathilde wasn't there yet. Fifteen minutes didn't really count as being late, especially for a girl. If she'd taken a taxi, she was probably stuck in traffic. Or in the métro if she'd taken the métro. Or else she was searching the neighborhood for the hotel. Maybe I should have suggested that we meet someplace that was easier to find. It's true that the hotel was really tiny and not at all easy to spot. I wasn't sure if "Hôtel du Quai Voltaire" was even written on the facade, so there you go.

I went to take a look at my bottle of champagne. The ice cubes in the bucket had nearly all melted. I took one and swallowed it. My stomach was aching more and more. The best thing would be to eat something. But I was still very surprised to not feel hungry. The truth is—and I'd prefer not to tell you this, but it's part of the story—I was really nervous at the idea of being in that room with Mathilde. I was afraid of being clumsy or inappropriate. Suddenly my cell rang. It crushed my heart. I said to myself: "No, no, no . . ." I was scared to death she was calling to cancel. The caller's name was blocked. I didn't want to pick up, in case it was someone I didn't want to talk to, like my mother or François. I waited nervously for the message beep, but it didn't come. No message. That put me over the top. What if it was Mathilde? Why didn't she leave me a message? I started to pace around the room. Damn. There was something about all this I didn't like. I figured the call must've been my mother again and that I shouldn't worry, Mathilde would be there soon. She'd said she had to go shopping with her father. She must've found an excuse to come over here. Obviously she'd been held up a little, that was all. But she was coming. Besides, why wouldn't she come? After all, she had taken my hand in the Jardin d'acclimatation. So she was coming. All I had to do was wait. I was sorry there was no television. A hotel room without a TV is like a woman without any legs: there's something missing. Even if they're all jerks on TV. But it makes waiting easier. I opened the window and leaned out to see if I could spot her walking along the sidewalk. The quais were really jammed. Traffic wasn't moving at all, except for the taxi lane, which was empty. The cars were bumper to bumper. To reassure myself, I thought that for all I knew, her father was going to drop her off, but they were running late because of the traffic. Let's say they'd gone shopping at Galeries Lafayette. Then, at around eight thirty, Mathilde asked him to drop her off in my neighborhood. At that time of night, with the traffic, it would take a lot more than half an hour to get to quai Voltaire. Then I imagined that one day there should be a quai Parme somewhere in Paris. That would be nice. People would walk along it on Sunday mornings, reciting some of my poems by heart. I wasn't too crazy about Voltaire. Madame Thomas had made us read some of his things. They were okay, but they didn't blow you away. I think a book is great when your throat hurts after you've read it. And that pain in your throat could be anxiety, or sadness, or any emotion that isn't a soft cushion that someone slips behind your back so you can sit more comfortably. You know what I mean.

Out on the Seine, the barges weren't sailing by anymore. It was probably too late. I once knew a girl whose uncle lived on a barge. Not in Paris, but nearby. She threw a kind of party on board once. I was trying to focus on all those memories so as not to think about Mathilde too much. From my point of view, waiting for someone who isn't coming is the worst kind of torture. I tried to remember the girl's name. And also the names of people I was with at the time. The thing with my mother was that we moved around a lot. So I changed schools often, which is why I don't really have any childhood friends. I tried to visualize every apartment I'd ever lived in. Then I came back to the idea that it was probably too late to see a barge sailing by. I would've liked to see one, I don't know why. Even though a barge isn't what you'd call something unusual. But I felt like seeing one, don't ask me why. Then I thought about all the seagulls that got fooled by following barges from Le Havre up to Paris. In the beginning they figured they'd found a good deal, because there's probably lots of stuff to eat on a barge. They were having a feast. So of course they followed the barges for a few days. Until they found themselves in Paris. And once they were there, I figure they must be unhappy. A seagull that is away from the sea must get depressed. Anyway, I was thinking all this pointless stuff so as not to think about Mathilde, but I wasn't succeeding, because the only thing I kept telling myself was that she was really late, and for all I knew she wasn't coming.

By now it was nearly ten o'clock. We were bound to miss the last show. But that was no big deal. A movie wasn't the main thing; we could skip it. I went to check the champagne bucket. There was nothing but water inside. For some reason, that shot my mood all to hell. At one point, I came within an inch of calling Marco to ask for Mathilde's number. For all I knew, her father hadn't let her go out again after yesterday's party. But if she didn't call, that meant she planned to come. That was for sure. So she was coming. But she could've called to tell me when, so I wouldn't go on pacing and stressing for nothing. That's why I thought of calling Marco. But I couldn't see myself talking to him, after what he pulled on me. Anyway, Marco was a snitch, so within three minutes everyone would know that Mathilde and I were planning to meet, which would screw everything up. It would be just like my mother to call Mathilde and ask where I was. She wouldn't find out, of course, but the idea of the two of them talking bothered me. I could already imagine my mother telling Mathilde what I'd done to Bénédicte. I suddenly felt incredibly uptight. She would tell her that I'd sent Bénédicte to the emergency room, and that I was violent. At first, Mathilde would have trouble believing it. You'd have trouble believing it, too. To look at me, you wouldn't think I was the kind of person to punch a girl. Even if somebody called me up one day to tell me that I'd hit a girl in the face, I wouldn't believe it myself. I would say: "I'm really sorry, pal, but that's impossible. I know him like I know myself and I'm telling you, he's not that way at all. Julien Parme is a poet. A poet, not a thug." The problem was that Mathilde would remember the line about Yann Chevillard that I'd fed her in the taxi. She'd also remember the cut on my face and the blood she'd seen. She'd start to think that I'd told her a bunch of bullshit, and that this story about my stepsister was probably true. She would also think that in fact, I was a real animal, a dangerous guy who would punch a girl in the face, which is sacred. I suddenly told myself all that, and got really scared that was what had happened. That was why she wasn't coming to our date.

I closed the window, then opened it again. I lit another menthol cigarette. I was starting to feel paranoid. She was going to come. I just had to be patient. To kill time, I went into the bathroom. I took some toilet paper, rolled it into balls, and then wet them so they would be harder, and nice and soggy. I went back to the window and practiced throwing them. It might have been fun to aim at a few passersby. But it was too dangerous; I would be spotted in nothing flat. So what I did was to throw them as far as I could. Just to see. Sometimes when you're waiting for something that isn't happening, you wind up doing stupid things like that, don't ask me why.

Suddenly I stopped, because of another thought I'd had. Maybe Mathilde had heard all about Madame Thomas and me. At the idea, a huge shiver went through me, I swear. How could she have found out? Marco wouldn't have said anything. It made me look too good, and if there's one thing Marco doesn't like, it's making other people look good, especially me. On the other hand, I could easily imagine that girl Alice phoning her pal Emilie Fermat to bawl her out for not waiting for us. And after that of course they would have told each other how the party ended, and all. Alice would have talked about me, for sure. I know girls. When they tell something, they can't resist going into detail. They just can't help themselves. Especially since in this case what Alice had to tell was really juicy. Like I was sleeping with my French teacher, and also that I'd touched her breast in the taxi. Emilie would repeat that to Mathilde right away, and it would totally turn her off to me.

I picked up the room telephone and pressed the button for the front desk. I asked the guy if anyone was waiting for me in the bar. He said he would go check, and I started feeling hopeful again, but he came back to say no. That did me in. So I asked him to ring my room if somebody asked for me. He said of course. And we hung up. The thing is, now I felt like vomiting. I went into the bathroom. I even kneeled over the toilet, if you want details. Just in case. But in the end I didn't really feel like it. I only managed to spit. So I went back to bed and leafed through my *Super Scrooge McDuck.* I had finished the big adventure in the middle, so I started reading a Mickey Mouse story. But I don't like the way Mickey Mouse looks.

Just then, I had a horrible intuition. It made me put down my comic book, because I couldn't concentrate on the stupid story: maybe Bénédicte had recognized Mathilde's purse when we met in Titan's stall. Mathilde had been riding Titan just before our fight, so Bénédicte may have figured out what I was doing at the club. She was sure to have spent hours wondering why I'd shown up there, and she must have figured it was for Mathilde. Who knows, maybe the two of them knew each other very well. Mathilde may not have realized that our parents lived together. After all, Bénédicte and I don't have the same last names. She's Bénédicte de Courtois; how could Mathilde connect her with me, Julien Parme? For all I knew, they often ran into each other at the club on Saturdays. Sometimes they would go riding together, and afterward they would clean their horses and tell each other about their lives. Girlfriends, in other words. Bénédicte was a little older. I could very well imagine her giving Mathilde a few tips, especially about competitions and all. I couldn't get over it. The more I thought about it, the more this version of events took hold in my mind. So Bénédicte would have called her to tell her what kind of a brute and little asshole I was, and Mathilde would have been convinced. I had told her a pack of lies. My story about Yann Chevillard was nothing but hot air. And she would suddenly understand that I was a violent guy, and all I wanted was to get her in a hotel room with me. That's why she'd decided not to keep our date. I scared her. It hadn't even occurred to her to tell me. And that kept running through my mind, and spinning off in every direction. I could see all the possibilities, and it made me sick.

At one point, I even imagined that she had revealed the address of my hotel. I was afraid I wasn't safe in my room anymore. The cops would've interrogated her and she would've told the truth. As proof, she still had the hotel stationery I'd given her so she'd have the exact address. I was starting to play movies in my head. For all I knew, the cops would show up any minute. I went to my window to check. I was starting to panic. Maybe it would be safer to leave the hotel right away. I seriously considered it, I swear. I was getting more nervous than I'd ever been in my life. Because I didn't have any idea of where I could go. And yet there were lots of possibilities. I could change hotels; there's no shortage of them in Paris. But I didn't feel like it. I was devastated just by the thought that Mathilde might have betrayed me. I didn't care about anything anymore. If I got caught there, it would be because she'd betrayed me, and if she'd betrayed me, I wouldn't have the heart to make a run for it in any case. I would let myself be taken, nice and easy. I wouldn't cause any trouble. The cops would knock on the door, and I'd let them take me away without saying anything. I'd keep quiet as I held out my wrists for the handcuffs. And I knew what to expect after that. They'd take me to the station, where I'd have to tell them everything. Then they might send me to a social worker or something, and they'd ask me to tell it all over again. That would go on for hours. And at the end they'd send me away someplace. To a boarding school, or to some special center for guys like me who have trouble dealing with life and who suddenly go out of control.

I went into the bathroom and threw up. It made my whole body sting. Then I started to cry. I swear. I didn't know why I was crying. The acid taste in my mouth had made me snap. The fatigue, too. After that I rinsed my face. I brushed my teeth, but without conviction. Then I went to bed. I thought back to the seagulls, wondering how they managed to live in Paris. That reminded me of the duckling at the Jardin d'acclimatation. I remembered what Mathilde had said. I should never have picked it up. So I imagined myself getting out of bed in the middle of the night and taking a cab back there. Once I was alone in front of the entrance, I would climb over the fence. Being very careful, since there was a lot of surveillance in the area. Once on the other side, I would start to run. But a light would come on behind me in the darkness. A kind of flashlight. The guard's. I would run at top speed. And a chase would start all through the park. Luckily I would be able to shake them, but just barely. Then I would find the place where I'd seen the little duckling. He would be hard to find in the darkness. I would have the hotel matches with me and I would light dozens of them, while I whispered, "Here, ducky-ducky," until I found him. I would pick him up very gently, with the idea of bringing him with me, and taking care of him. But that's when I would discover that he didn't look like himself anymore. Or that he looked like an old sock. Like he'd been attacked by another duck. Or by his mother, for all I knew. In any case one thing was sure: he would be dead. Already dead.

I started to yawn. It must have been eleven o'clock. I was all in. I hadn't realized how beat I was. I even had trouble keeping my eyes open. I didn't get undressed, in case Mathilde showed up. At one point I imagined that her father had forbidden her to go out. After all, she had gone to sleep past two o'clock in the morning the night before. She would pretend to obey, and would go to bed right after dinner. But actually she would've prepared a little bag with a few essentials in it. I could imagine her taking a book along. That would be like her. Maybe a novel. Then she would sneak out. It would already be midnight. Once outside, she would take a taxi to come to me. She would be afraid that I was already asleep. At the front desk, she would ask for my room number. She would go upstairs. And I would hear her little fingers knocking on the door. This version was actually more like Mathilde. Because after all, she was the person who took my hand on a kiddie ride. She was the one who told me the story about her sister running away, to cheer me up. Yes, her little fingers on the door to my room. I had to keep my clothes on. Just in case. Even if I knew very well that she wasn't coming. And that for all I knew I would never see her again in my life. Never.

At that, I fell asleep.

Chapter 20

I woke up pretty early, and immediately switched on my phone. It was nine thirty. I had another message from my mother. This time, I listened to it. She sounded strange. She said she was at the emergency room with Bénédicte, and that I better be home when she got back. The call was from last night. No news from Mathilde, on the other hand. Then I went right down to get some breakfast, and ate like I was starving. I told the front desk I would probably be staying an extra night, but that was a lie. Up in my room, I got my things together. I didn't have much. I took my magazines; I didn't want anyone to find them later. I put my letter to Madame Morozvitch in an envelope. It would make her happy. I took a last look around before leaving the room. The sight of the bottle of champagne in its bucket depressed me.

I went straight to the Gare de Lyon. I first thought of going by bus, because the weather was really nice, but it was Sunday, and buses on Sunday are like the women you love: you can wait for them forever. So I went by métro. Since I was a little early,

I walked around the station. Then I went to buy my ticket for Rome. Holding the ticket in my hand really felt like something, I swear. Now I was really going to be able to make it out of here. At the Maison de la Presse, I wanted to buy some magazines, but wound up getting a novel instead. There were tons of them for sale. I figured it probably wouldn't be a masterpiece. Novels for sale in train stations are usually train-station novels, if you know what I mean—badly written stuff. Still, I felt like reading one. After hesitating for a long time, I chose *Steppenwolf* by Hermann Hesse, because of the title. I also bought a stamp and looked around for a mailbox, but when I finally found one, I wasn't sure what to do. After all, was Madame Morozvitch even able to read? Reading is never easy for blind people. Even though I had my doubts about her dark glasses, as I told you. At worst, someone would read it aloud to her, the way I used to read her letters from her son in the old days. For all I knew, her son would read her the letter. The thought made me feel really lousy. I didn't want anyone to know I was going to Italy, especially not that asshole. I stood motionless in front of the mailbox for a few minutes, and finally threw my letter into a trash can. Then I went to wait in front of the departure board. The train for Lausanne was on Track 12. Once I got to Lausanne, I had a five-hour layover, and then I would take a sleeper to Rome. Sleeping cars are too cool. I've loved them ever since I was little. Just the fact of sleeping on a train makes you feel you're going very far away. Before heading to Track 12, I sat down on a café terrace across from the platforms. I wanted apricot juice, but they didn't have any, so I settled for orange juice. I watched the people passing by. Most of them were leaving. They were dragging huge suitcases. I even saw a guy with skis. That surprised me, it being April. But some mountains are apparently so high that you can ski all year long. My father told me that and I've often heard it since, so it must be true.

I had nearly two hours ahead of me, so I started reading the novel. It was really good. In the beginning it was the story of a man who had two halves: he was both a wolf and a man. That was the metaphor that Hermann Hesse had come up with to show craziness. Because the hero's basic problem was that he was crazy. Every time he did something, the wolf inside of him bared its teeth. And each time the wolf inside him drove him to do certain things, the man was sorry and blamed himself. In short, there was always a conflict going on inside him. After that, the man met a woman in a jazz bar. She was really alive, and all. The proof was that in addition to liking music, she loved to dance. She was the one who would reconcile him with life. That's what the novel was saying. I thought it was terrific, especially the writing and what it said about life. If you ask me, Voltaire should have read it before sitting down to write his silly tales.

I thought about Mathilde again. I couldn't understand why she hadn't gotten in touch with me. That was a real mystery. I ran through all the possibilities in my head, but wearily. Basically it was like the empty study that was lit up every night: you can search for explanations and build theories, but you'll never come up with one that will let you definitely say "This is it" or "That's it." In any case one thing was sure: she had shot me down. But as I thought about it, I realized she hadn't told anyone the address of my hotel, either. She could have. Somebody else might have. That would've been horrible. But no, she had respected that. For all I knew, she was standing at her bedroom window at her father's at this very moment, looking out at the scene she'd shown me. Across the way, the lights in the study were out. And she was saying to herself that I must be at the station, getting ready to leave for Italy. She would imagine me the way I was, on a café terrace thinking about her and about the train I was going to take any moment now. She was the only person who knew about Italy. And she must realize that, at her bedroom window. That we shared that secret. At the thought, I realized I was happy. I felt light. I can't explain it. I was thinking that she hadn't completely betrayed me, in the end. She hoped I would realize that. Something had come up that kept her from meeting me, but she hoped I would understand that it wasn't a betrayal, not really.

Then I started to daydream about Italy. I'd been rereading the same page in my book for the last ten minutes. I was lost in my thoughts. I had enough cash to get through the next few days. After that, I would manage. I was sure to find something. And if I didn't, I would take a train to Nice. I would explain everything to my uncle. He would understand. In a word, life would go on. You could even say that life was starting now. I'd had trouble getting free of all my hassles, but now I was on my way. I looked up from my book. There was a gigantic clock on the right. The train was leaving in ten minutes. But I wanted to wait until the last moment before getting up. So I went back to my reading. The passage I was trying to finish was great. The hero meets a Spanish musician who gives him some cigarettes, but they're special and they allow him to take off into real deliriums inside himself. When you smoke this drug you find yourself in a kind of big hallway with lots of doors. And behind each door is something that will completely change your personality. At one point the hero meets Mozart, whom he worships. If I could go down that hallway, I'm sure I'd come face to face with La Fontaine behind one of the doors. We would have a little literary chat, him and me. Nice and quiet, between friends. I would tell him that honestly, nobody had written anything as good as the *Fables* since his death, and that we studied them this year with Madame Thomas. He would listen to me carefully. La Fontaine is an attentive guy. Then he would offer me something to drink. Like tea. Or apricot juice, because that turns out to be his favorite juice, too. And suddenly, just as I'm telling him about the novel I want to write, which I will call *Apricot Juice*, he would ask me if I'm planning to take my train to Rome. There he pulls a clock out from under his shirt. No kidding, a clock. That's not usually possible, I know. But this is La Fontaine, the greatest writer in the world. And you can clearly see from the clock that I only have three minutes before the train was going to take off. "I know, I know," I answer, feeling really relaxed. It's time to go. But what Jean doesn't know is how fast I can run. Between the tortoise and the hare, it's no contest. To go from the café where I'm sitting daydreaming to Track 12 takes me less than a minute. So I still have two more minutes. And when you've dreamed of meeting La Fontaine all your life, two extra minutes matter. Then he suggests that we go for a little walk. Just a quick one. And he takes me by the arm. Just two writers. We walk that way down the famous hallway, looking at the animals. We stop in front of a door. I have no idea what's behind it. So he tells me to open it, to see. I do, and I find myself in a strange, very bright room. Bénédicte is lying on a bed with all sorts of tubes stuck in her. A nurse walks up to explain that she was attacked by a herd of elephants and that she's in a coma.

"In a coma?" I react right away. "No, we just had a little argument, that's all. She must be pretending. I know her. She's a bitch. She always pretends, to make you feel guilty."

"No, no. She's in a coma, I tell you. A light coma, but still. An entire herd ran over her."

I turn to Jean to see what he thinks of this, but he has disappeared. I call to him: "Jean! Jean!" but nobody answers. Staying in this depressing room makes me heartsick. I go back out to the hallway, but I still can't find him. I start to panic. I'm running every which way. In the hallway, all the doors are locked except one. I open it. If you'd seen me, I wasn't looking too sharp. You could hear a loudspeaker blaring at top volume: "Only one minute left! Only one minute!" I know it has to do with my train, but I pretend not to understand. Okay. I push open the door. It's the door to my apartment, I recognize it right away, and I find myself facing my mother. I remember the story Mathilde told me about her sister running away. When she came back, her father cried and took her in his arms, and told her never to do that to him again. But that isn't possible for me, because of Bénédicte who might be in a coma. So I start feeling incredibly bad about hitting her. I would've wanted to take it back, but it's too late. What's done is done. For that matter, that's one of the reasons why life is a trap that we all fall into sooner or later.

Sitting there in the great hall of the Gare de Lyon, I looked up from my novel. I'm out of my mind, I thought. Completely out of my mind. Whenever I read something, I start daydreaming, and I reread the same page seventy-six times in a row. The train was going to leave at any moment, but I couldn't stop reading my book. I only had ten pages left, so I went on reading. "I have to finish it before I take my train," I told myself. "I have to." It was the first time I'd read an entire book in one sitting. Ten pages isn't a big deal, except that each page was an excuse for daydreaming. But I made an effort to focus, to finish it as quickly as possible. I could already see myself jumping up at the last word and running, you know, running like a rabbit, and boarding the train one second before the door closed. I would go sit down and it would take at least ten minutes for me to catch my breath and for my heart to slow down a little. Then I would lean my forehead against the train window and watch the landscape roll by, slowly at first, then faster and faster.

It would really feel like something. "Good-bye, cruel world," I would say to myself. Pretty emotional, anyway. As luck would have it, there would be some really beautiful Swiss girl across from me who was going skiing in the mountains with eternal snows and all. I would recite a couple of La Fontaine's fables to impress her. Like the one about the frog who pretended to be as big as a cow. After four hours of chatting, she would be charmed and would suggest I spend a few days with her and her family in the Alps. That sort of thing can happen, you never know. Or else I would go on leaning my forehead against the window and look at the Paris suburbs and then the country-side, with fields and sheep, and farms. And I would feel life starting for me at last. Real life.

I put my book down and got to my feet. I was in no hurry. The train had long since gone. I left some money for my or-ange juice. I was holding my ticket in my hand. I looked at it. I also looked over at the empty platform. I stood there for a moment without moving, thoughtful and solemn, like a moun-tain climber who has reached the top of Mont Blanc, but who knows that his destiny must be to climb back down eventually.

Then I turned around. I walked out of the station. I took a taxi. On the way, I started to cry, but just a little. My stomach ached. It hurt bad when my tears ran over my cut. So much the better, I thought; I deserved it. I even dug my nails into my wrist to hurt myself more. I thought of my father.

I thought about him for a long time.

When we reached my building, I got out of the taxi. I dried my tears. I keyed in the door code. Okay. I stepped into the entryway, my soul trembling. To give myself courage, I thought back to the story that Mathilde had told me about her sister. I imagined my mother taking me in her arms like that, crying and telling me never to do this to her again. If that miracle happened, I would never do this again, for sure. Ever. I would learn to live right and behave myself. I would stop lying.

I took a deep breath to drive away my fear. And I took the elevator, hoping very hard that she would forgive me. Forgive me for being who I was, and not someone else.